, Howard, '

on the

Scotch on the Rocks

Scotch
on the Rocks

Howard Browne

ST. MARTIN'S PRESS

New York

Design by Susan Hood

Library of Congress Cataloging-in-Publication Data
Browne, Howard
        Scotch on the rocks / Howard Browne.
            p.   cm.
        ISBN 0-312-05509-9
        I. Title.
PS3503.R8436S29   1991
813'.54—dc20   90-49000
                                       CIP

First Edition: February 1991

1   3   5   7   9   10   8   6   4   2

R00803   24002

In loving memory of
DORIS ELLEN BROWNE

Texas

—✕—

June 1932

1

*T*hey were wearing their Sunday best. As Emily Dawson had said at five that morning, over breakfast, "Just 'cause we're bein' made poor, don't mean we hafta *look* poor."

Now she stood, along with her son and his wife, on the front porch of their small white farmhouse, holding her chin high and her shoulders squared, watching in stony silence as the family possessions went under the hammer.

The foreclosure sale had started promptly at nine. By noon, with the livestock already sold off and driven or hauled away, bids were being asked on farm implements and machinery by Mr. Tolliver, the auctioneer.

Mr. Tolliver was a small man, neatly put together, with delicate features, a surprisingly deep voice, and black hair worn slicked back and parted in the center. Since the stock market crash nearly three years earlier, his services were more and more in demand by banks as the Depression deepened and the number of foreclosures and bankruptcies increased. In place of a business suit, he wore overalls and a field hand's straw hat: camouflage against being linked with those who employed him.

"Now, folks," he said briskly. "I want to offer for your consideration this here fine, practic'ly brand-new *De*Laval cream separator. The best money can buy, even secondhand can't be had these days under less'n sixty dollars, now do I hear fifty?"

A woman in a faded blue linsey-woolsey dress called out, "Fi' dollars."

The day was gray and overcast, with no hint of badly needed rain. Loosely grouped about the auctioneer were perhaps thirty men and women, many in overalls and house dresses. They stood stoically in the powdery gray dust of the Dawsons' front yard, silent, numbly aware that what was taking place here today might well be in store for many of them before the summer was over.

Lapsing smoothly into his auctioneer's chant, Mr. Tolliver said, "Five dollars the bid, I got five dollars bid, do I hear ten, who'll make it ten, real bargain here, folks, ten, ten, do I hear ten?"

A man's voice called out, "Seven."

"Thank you, sir," Mr. Tolliver said. "Seven dollars bid, now do I hear fifteen?"

Early on, Mr. Tolliver had spotted the familiar faces of two "vultures" in the crowd: secondhand dealers from Corpus Christi who made a practice of attending foreclosure sales throughout the county. One of the pair called out, "Twelve."

Ambrose Dawson said, "Shit!"

His mother glared at him. "Brose! I will not abide that kinda talk!"

Ambrose said thickly, "Can't stomach it, Maw. Close on twenty years doin' business with George Willis's bank, yet he up and sells us out. For two red cents I'd hunt down the old son of a bitch and use the shotgun on him."

"Hush!" Emily Dawson said. "The good Lord in His wisdom has seen fit to test our faith, and we must endure it."

With the cream separator knocked down on a final bid of twenty-four dollars by one of the men from Corpus Christi, Mr. Tolliver moved on to a cotton-sledder near the now empty corral and asked for an opening bid. But since weevils and lack of rain during the past two years had wiped out most of the southern Texas cotton crop, there was no response.

Mr. Tolliver switched to the next item. "Now, folks," he began, "like to call your attention to this here horse-drawn disc harrow. Bradley make, twenty discs with scrapers, give you a ten-foot cut. Gonna run you fifty—sixty-five dollars, today's prices. Who'll start her off at forty?"

Ruby Dawson had stopped listening. All it added up to was just one more lousy break to prove she'd been *born* snakebit. From the day she'd first walked into a schoolhouse wearing a neighbor kid's hand-me-downs, nothing had gone right. Although she was bright, energetic, and more than passably pretty, her caustic tongue and an ingrained go-to-hell attitude had kept her classmates at a distance. Failure to make friends, the certainty that everyone regarded her as a freak, plus a brief affair with a married forty-year-old teacher had led to her dropping out of high school during her junior year.

At eighteen, fed up with making beds and emptying slop jars at her mother's rooming house, Ruby packed a bag and walked out for good. Over the next five years she worked as a waitress in a succession of roadside diners, beaneries, and restaurants throughout much of southeast Texas. She was more at ease with the clientele and employees of such places; no one upstaged her, her private life went uncensured. Friendships, although superficial, were easy to establish. During those years she had gone through several affairs, none lasting more than a few months before sputtering out.

Ruby was twenty-three when Ambrose Dawson first showed up at the Lazy Boy diner in Corpus Christi late one summer evening in 1928. He was thirty-six, a tall, rawboned man whom Ruby first mistook for the Hollywood actor Tim McCoy. He'd taken a seat at her station and, it being a slow night and all, they'd got to talking. He told her about his owning this farm and how, back six years, a horse had kicked

5

his wife to death two weeks after the wedding. The next night he'd come in again, got around to asking her to go to a picture show with him. Two nights after that they ended up in bed; a week later they were married.

Now, with them losing everything, Ruby faced the bitter realization that she'd likely end up right back where she started: waiting on tables in some hash house. Supporting herself—*and* her husband *and* his mother. Least till Brose could find him a job—and, what with half the country out of work, that could take till doomsday.

Earlier, Mr. Tolliver and his helper had set out most of the household furnishings in the south yard to make room for the crowd. With the farm implements either sold or passed over entirely by the bidders, the auctioneer turned to the smaller items.

"Now first thing we got here," Mr. Tolliver said, "is something bound to interest you ladies. And that's this dandy, hardly used sewing machine. Franklin brand, foot-powered, goes for something like fifty dollars, new. Do I hear thirty?"

2

*H*is name was Leonard Valigurski, alias Lawrence Vaughn, alias Leon Vernon, alias Leland Vickers.

As of now, he was calling himself Lee Vance.

He was a tall, slender man, dark-haired, sleekly handsome, a year past thirty. At the moment he was wearing a three-piece charcoal gray suit with a thin white stripe. His shirt was white-on-white Madras, his necktie blue silk with a subdued pattern of gray fleur-de-lis, his shoes black and white oxfords, his socks gray silk with blue clocks, his straw hat a Panama import.

In New York City, his wardrobe would barely have drawn a second glance. In Corpus Christi, among the overalls, Levis, Stetsons, and cowboy boots set, it made him conspicuous. Even a shade ridiculous.

It was the exact impression Lee Vance sought to give.

The bellhop said, "Well, sir, Mr. Vance, I guess that's gotta depend on what you lookin' for. Now if it's wimmen . . . there's Miz Wilson, runs this real nice place over on . . ."

Lee put up a silencing hand, said, "What I had more in mind were games of chance. Dice, poker, perhaps roulette. Something along those lines."

The bellhop frowned. "Well, we got this rest'runt out the enda Jefferson. I ain't claimin' to know all that much about it, but I hear as how they got some action goin' on in one'a the back rooms out there."

"Afraid that's not for me," Lee said. "Place like that, there's always the chance of running into crooked dice or some card shark dealing off the bottom of the deck. Or whatever it is they do to cheat."

Acutely aware of the five-spot Lee was idly twisting between his fingers, the bellhop said, "Jeez, I sure wish I could help you there, Mr. Vance. . . . A'course there *is* this here private game goes on upstairs Sataday nights. But I never heard of 'em lettin' no outsiders in."

Lee Vance handed over the banknote. "This private game. Tell me about it."

Anthony "Tony Large" Malino, five-nine, 230 pounds, a graudate cum laude of Baylor University, said, "You'll only be using back roads. Not that the Rangers will present a problem; that'll be taken care of beforehand. But—although it's hardly likely considering the time and route—you may run into the sheriff's men."

Sal Calucci said, "What about we do bump into them guys?"

"Going there, you've nothing to be concerned about," Malino said. "On the way back . . ." He made an abrupt, thumbs-down gesture more chilling than words. "But only if that can't be avoided." He smiled. "After all, this is not Chicago."

That last sentence drew appreciative grins. "Anyway," Malino said, "it'll come to around ninety miles round trip. When the time comes, I'll give the word to Cheech he's to be behind the wheel. There and back."

Seth Abbott, a newcomer to the Malino organization, said, "Where'bouts we makin' this pickup?"

Malino turned suddenly cold eyes on him. "That's none of your fucking business. Clear?"

Abbott shrank back in his chair. "Jeez, boss, I was just askin'."

Malino said, "Let's say I was to tell you. Ahead of time. You have a few drinks, do a little careless talking—and the operation goes sour. That would mean I'd have to put all the blame on you, now wouldn't I?"

*T*he minute the young man came through the door, Elmer Cawthra, DDS, had him sized up as a big city boy. And, to judge from the silly outfit he was wearing, likely from a long way above the Mason-Dixon line.

They shook hands. Lee Vance said, "I certainly do appreciate your giving me an appointment on such short notice, Dr. Cawthra."

"You wanta know the God's truth, Mr. Vance," Cawthra drawled, "times bein' what they are, I'm not that all-fired busy to begin with. These days, seems folks don't wanta waste what little money they got on teeth-fixin'." He indicated the dental chair. "Now you just plant your backside right there, Mr. Vance, and let me in on what your problem might be."

Lee sat down, tugged his trouser legs up an inch or two to protect their knife-edge crease, and leaned back. "Actually, nothing at all urgent, Dr. Cawthra. The company I'm with has been keeping me on the road here the last few months and I've had to miss my regular checkup. And since I have a couple of days layover in your city . . ."

Draping a protective cloth about his patient's neck, Cawthra said, "You don't mind my askin', Mr. Vance, what line'a work might you be in?"

"Sales," Lee told him. "Out of Chicago." He fished a business card from a vest pocket.

The balding, middle-aged dentist squinted at the embossed lettering, grunted, handed it back. "Wholesale hardware, huh? How's business?"

"Matter of fact," Lee said, "it's not all that good. The company bought out this barbed-wire manufacturer a few months back. I'm down here to introduce the product."

The dentist removed a metal mouth-mirror and a probe from a sterilizer. "You sure picked one piss-poor time to peddle bobwire. Least 'round these parts. We got us a *de*pression goin' on down here, mister, anyone was to up and ask you. Open wide."

After a brief examination, Cawthra straightened, put aside the instruments. He said, "Little tartar buildup s'all. And far's I can make out, there's no leaks 'round them two silver fillings you got in there. Say the word and I'll rid you'a that tartar."

"Might as well," Lee said. "As long as I'm here."

Between necessary pauses, the conversation continued. Politics came up and, once it was established that Lee was a staunch Methodist, Cawthra said no question, Hoover had to go, but that he just didn't know about this "crippled fella" Roosevelt.

"From what I been hearin'," he said, "man's real name's Rosenfeld—somethin' like that. That'd make him one'a them New York Jews. Wouldn't set well this parta the country."

Lee smiled. "A Jew, eh? Can't you just see cousin Teddy Roosevelt come charging out of a synagogue yelling 'Bully!' on his way up San Juan Hill? No; go back far enough and I think you'll find the family's Dutch."

"Folks musta plumb forgot about him bein' related to ol' Teddy," Cawthra said. "Irregardless, whoever gets the job sure's gotta be better'n this shitheel we got in there now."

He dropped the tools back into the sterilizer, whipped away the protective cloth. "That's gonna do it, Mr. Vance. And if I do say so myself, no fancy Chicago dentist coulda done any better for you."

Lee left the chair, brushed a few flakes of lint from his lapel. He said, "What do I owe you, Doctor?"

"Three dollars sound about right to you?"

Waiting for change from a five, Lee said casually, "I find weekends in an unfamiliar town to be quite a bore. You wouldn't happen to know of some way I could . . . liven up the next day or two?"

Cawthra handed over two singles peeled from a sizable roll. "Right offhand I'd have to tell you, no sir. I don't. Most travelin' men I bump into do seem interested in the ladies. That case, I might mention Clara Wilson's house on West Guthrie."

Lee smiled. "It so happens I'm a happily married man, Doctor. Two fine children. No, my vice is limited to dealing the pasteboards. Preferably contract bridge. Or rummy. And if I should happen to get pushed into it, I can always find my way around a poker table."

Cawthra lifted an eyebrow. "Poker, hey? Well, seein' as how you happen to be a patient'a mine, I just might be able to he'p you out on that."

For a total outlay of eight dollars, five of that to the hotel bellhop, Lee Vance had maneuvered himself into position to make a killing.

3

*I*t was close to nine o'clock before Emily Dawson, aided by the light of a full moon, finished loading the Ford station wagon with items salvaged from the foreclosure sale. After her son had secured the more bulky items to the car roof, she and Ruby had set about cramming much of the interior with blankets, towels, clothing, kitchen utensils, and tableware, along with fourteen mason jars of homemade jellies and preserves, a fifteen-pound smoked ham butt, and several loaves of freshly baked bread wrapped in damp cloth.

Ambrose, back to wearing overalls and a work shirt, had finally protested. "Gonna look like we're a buncha Okies, Maw. We're headin' for Christi, not China. What's Ben gonna think, us showin' up loaded down with all this here food?"

"Seein' as how there'll be three extra mouths to feed for the good Lord knows how long," Emily said tartly, "Ruth Proudfit'll welcome ever' bit we can bring. Bad enough, them havin' to take us in like it was charity. And I'll thank you to say no more about it."

Noticing his somber expression, her tone softened. "It's turnin' late, Brose. You fixin' to be on the road come sunup, better git y'self straight to bed."

"Yeah, Maw," Ambrose Dawson said absently. "I'm gonna do that."

Aware of how deeply he was troubled, Emily put a soothing

hand on his arm. "Son, losin' the farm and all ain't the enda the world. Long as we hold onto our faith in the goodness of the Lord, He will provide."

Ambrose gave her a twisted smile. "Sure wouldn't count on it none. Seems here the last couple'a years the old gentleman's gone pure Republican on us."

Emily jerked her hand away. "Bite your tongue, young man! God is not mocked."

She left him there and returned to the house. He drew a folder of rice papers and a Bull Durham sack from his shirt pocket, rolled himself a cigarette, used a kitchen match to set it burning, then walked slowly over to the empty corral and stood there, resting a foot on the bottom rail.

He'd been born here. In that back bedroom, the bedroom he and Ruby shared to this day. A second had been added shortly after his twin sisters were born. They had died within hours of each other three years later, victims of diphtheria. He was only eight at the time, but he still clearly remembered his mother at the burial, straight-backed and dry-eyed, her lips moving in silent prayer, while clods of clay thudded hollowly against those two small raw pine coffins.

Thoughts crowded in. What'd happened to all them big ideas he'd come up with after his daddy died back in '27? Like taking out a loan to buy old man Gooch's sixty acres when he'd kicked off. And fixing up some kinda generator so's there'd be 'lectric lights 'steada coal-oil lamps and a radio you didn't have to keep feeding batteries to. A real washing machine that didn't take pumping by hand. Ruby had nagged after him on all that, but he'd kept putting it off. But then what the hell, the bank woulda got it all by now, along with everything else in sight. . . .

The corral gate was standing open. Absently, he closed and secured it, achingly aware that there was nothing left to pen up, large or small. The chicken coops stood empty, there hadn't been a cat around the place for more'n a year now, and Rover, the basset hound, had been put down seven months back, so old and ailing the poor bastard couldn't lift up his head to lick your hand.

He stepped on the cigarette stub, ran a hand along the corral's top rail, then drifted over to the open barn door. A kerosene lamp hung from a nail; he took it down, lit the wick and entered the barn.

Empty. Nothing on God's earth could be emptier. Even the stink of animal shit seemed to have slacked off some since morning. He set the lamp on a broken milking stool and moved deeper into the barn. A faint scurrying sound from somewhere in back brought on a sour smile. Least the fucking mice hadn't up and quit on him.

From behind him, Ruby said, "You gonna just hang around out here or you comin' to bed?"

He turned. She was standing in the doorway, wrapped in a faded flannel nightgown under a man's checkered mackinaw, the pom-pom missing from one of her bedroom slippers.

He said, "*What* bed? Last I seen, it was high-tailin' off down the road. On the back enda Ross Dobkin's wagon."

"Don't matter," she said. "We still got them mattresses."

They stood there staring at each other. Today their world had ended; tomorrow had no paths, no signposts, no landmarks. Not something to be put into words, no hint of self-pity, though worry and frustration were cutting inside them like dull knives.

"You git up," Ruby said, "you better shave. Bad enough we hafta go beggin' for charity 'thout lookin' like somethin' the cat drug in."

Ambrose's face darkened. "Charity, my ass! I know Ben Proudfit ever since him an' me use to smoke cubabs out backa this here barn. Ben'd be honest-to-God hurt we wasn't to put up with him. Least till I git me somethin' to do."

"He's got a wife," Ruby said, "two kids and four rooms. How's he gonna feel after maybe a month or more and us still there?"

"Won't be nowhere that long. Man wants work bad enough, he's gonna find it."

"Don't you wish," Ruby said. "You try listenin' to somethin' on the radio 'sides 'Amos and Andy,' you'd know better. Even young fellas, way things is, can't hardly find work nowadays."

Unwittingly or not, she'd landed a low blow. His voice deceptively calm, Ambrose said, "You figger an old man like me can't git him a payin' job, huh, Ruby?"

She saw the look in his eyes and involuntarily took a step back. "Nobody's sayin' you're old."

Unappeased, he said, "Too damn bad you didn't thinka that backa ways. 'Fore you married some old fart like me."

"You shut your mouth!" Ruby said hotly. "I never once . . ."

He wasn't listening. " 'Ceptin' how many wet-eared snot-noses you run into coulda give you a house to live in and put clothes on your back?"

Furious, Ruby's voice turned shrill. "You sayin' I married you to git me a house? Somebody'd buy me clothes? Like I was some kinda . . . *gold* digger?"

"Sure's hell sounded like . . . "

"Well, you're all wet! First time I laid eyes on you, you had a shave and a shoeshine and you didn't act like a two-bit tip give you the right to talk dirty to a girl had to wait tables for a livin'. And you smelt like you took a bath more'n once a month and you held my arm crossin' the street and you didn't start grabbin' at my tits minute we was alone. Then I go and find out you're good in bed and want to marry me. So I did, house or no house, and you can go straight to hell!"

By the time she finished, Ambrose, his anger gone, was

grinning at her. He snaked an arm around her waist, said softly, "C'mere, you."

"Git away from me! Callin' me a gold digger."

He drew her close, grinning wolfishly. "Good in bed, huh? Lemme ask you somethin', kiddo. What good's a man that's good in bed if he ain't got a bed to be good in?"

Suddenly aware of what he was leading up to, Ruby made a halfhearted effort to pull away. Ambrose tightened his grip. "Know somethin', honey? Only thing didn't git sold off is all that nice sweet-smellin' hay we got waitin' for us up in the loft."

"You quit that," Ruby said firmly. "Too cold up there. 'Sides, you got any idea what time it's gettin' to be?"

His grin widened. "Now what's that got to do with the price'a aigs?"

By this time he had backed her to the base of the ladder leading up to the haymow. "Start climbin', honey. 'Fore I flop you right here on the floor."

"You crazy? I'm not gonna . . . "

"Sez you!" He chuckled deep in his throat. "You know damn well you want it bad's I do."

Abruptly, he ran his free hand up under her nightgown, smothering her squeal of outrage with his lips.

When he finally lifted his head and looked into her eyes, she was smiling.

4

*P*romptly at nine that night, Lee Vance and Dr. Elmer Caw-thra entered one of the luxury suites on the top floor of the Bayview Hotel.

A circular game table covered in green baize took up much of the center of the richly furnished living room. Near a side wall a kitchen table had been converted into a well-stocked bar. An end table next to a couch covered in gold damask held an oscillating fan, set up to dispel cigar and cigarette fumes.

Introductions were made, hands shaken. Of the four earlier arrivals, Clark Warren was the one who stood out: a semi-retired rancher, sixty, six-three, a shade over two hundred pounds, affable, with a booming voice, a hearty laugh, skin the color and texture of saddle leather. He pumped Lee's hand, said, "Right nice meetin' you, Mr. Vance. Doc, here, tells me you're a drummer? Some big hardware outfit back East?"

"Hibbard Spencer Bartlett," Lee said. "Chicago."

"Sure 'nough? Why, say, I hearda them." He pointed a thumb at the bottles on the makeshift bar. "If I'm correct in assumin' you're a drinkin' fella—and I never yet met a trav-elin' man wasn't—whyn't you fix you'self a libation. 'Fore we git settled down, do us some serious card-playin'."

Lee put a bourbon highball together and took the last of

the six straight-backed upholstered chairs at the table. Coats were removed and draped across chair backs, ties loosened, shirt sleeves rolled up. Clark Warren finished lighting a cigar, broke the seal on a pack of playing cards, removed the two jokers, set the deck aside.

He said, " 'Fore we start off, Mr. Vance—Lee?—lemme fill you in, the hows and wherefores. Win, lose or draw we quit at three A.M. Man runs outta cash, he's outta the game an' gits the job emptyin' ashtrays an' mixin' drinks.

"Now as to the kinda poker we're 'customed to playin' here. Mostly stud, five- or seven-card, though nobody's gonna object all that much to straight draw. No deuces wild, any'a that fancy shit. Dealer's choice, two-buck ante, ten-buck limit, raise to your little heart's content. 'Nother words, steep enough to keep out the sharecroppers. Whatta you say?"

Lee smiled, turned up his palms. "I say let's play us some poker, Mr. Warren."

"Make that Clark," Warren said. "Long's you're out to take a man's money, least you can do is use his front name."

A pause while wallets came out of pockets. Greenbacks were brought to light and neatly stacked, liquor glasses and ashtrays placed within easy reach. Clark Warren shuffled the deck thoroughly and expertly, then flipped a card, face up, to each player.

Amos Purcell, a thin-lipped, dour grocer in his late fifties, was the first to deal. Once the cards were mixed and cut and each player anted the required two dollars, Purcell said, "Stud, seven cards."

During the first half hour, Lee folded most hands early on. He lost a modest pot when Cawthra filled an inside straight, abandoned split tens when Purcell's fourth card turned out to be a second king, was handed a forty-two-dollar gift when Dale Bowers, head teller of the West Side Trust & Savings

Bank and thirty pounds overweight, made a foolish try for a spade flush on his last two cards.

It was in other ways that those thirty minutes paid off. He learned that the other players were careless when it came to exposing discards and failed hands, that Frank Dellacorte, an elderly, frail-bodied furniture dealer, could usually be bluffed into folding anything less than a high three-of-a-kind; that Clark Warren, regardless of the odds, backed his hunches to the limit; and that unless Bowers swore off poker in favor of mah-jongg or Parcheesi, he would likely end up absconding with a healthy chunk of his bank's assets.

It was Amos Purcell who could turn out to be a problem. The tight bloodless line of his lips and the built-in scowl told the world that here's a man with a suspicious mind. Not to mention a pair of darting, beady eyes that could likely spot a pimple on a gnat's ass.

At one-seventeen that morning, Tony Large was saying, "Go another two point three miles past that and you'll come to this dirt road on your left. Follow it till you reach this line of red oaks. Circle in behind it, pull up at the water's edge. Be there between three-thirty and four. No earlier, no later."

Cheech Fannelli said, "I'll make it okay, Mr. Malino. 'Less a'course this truck goes and breaks down on me. Somethin' like that."

"See that it doesn't," Tony Large said.

The two men were seated in the cab of a 1931 two-ton Diamond T truck. It was painted coal black, with a hooped, heavy black tarpaulin cover, and was capable of transporting a six-ton cargo. At the moment, its load consisted of eight tightly wired bales of alfalfa.

Tony Large said, "Pick up Sal and Patsy. This new man—Abbott—will be with them. The boat crew'll give you a hand with the load. Shouldn't take more than half an hour, if that. Those alfalfa bales are to be used as cover."

He opened the passenger door, stepped out, said, "I'll expect you back at the warehouse by six. At the latest."

The door slammed shut and Tony Large moved off along the sidewalk. Fannelli muttered, "Yes sir, *Mister* Malino."

After four hours, Lee had won slightly over four hundred dollars. Warren was well ahead, Purcell about even, Cawthra and Dellacorte each out a few hundred, leaving Bowers down by well over seven hundred.

At twenty past two, Clark Warren showed his three treys, drew in a thirty-dollar pot. He yawned hugely, said, "All night settin' here 'thout enough action to wake a fuckin' canary up. Coulda done better stayin' home, playin' Old Maid with the missus."

"Looks to me," Frank Dellacorte said, "you're doing all right."

Warren riffled his stack of bills, said, "Wouldn't call mebbe six hundred worth braggin' on. Least not when it comes to some'a them wild'n woolly nights we had us right at this here table."

He stood up abruptly, strode over to the bar and mixed a bourbon and water. He took a fresh deck of cards from the end table drawer, returned to his chair, sampled his drink, lit his third cigar of the night.

He said, "Your deal, Doc," and dropped the unopened pack in front of Cawthra. "See if you can mebbe coax a little git-up'n-go outta them."

Lee's turn to deal came twenty-three minutes before the game was scheduled to end. After the cut, he fed Bowers king-five as hole cards and an open king; Cawthra, a bust; Warren, sixes buried and an ace up; Dellacorte, split treys with a queen showing; Purcell, a nine; Lee, hidden eights and the four of spades showing.

"Ace bets," he said.

Warren tossed in two fives. Dellacorte called, as did Lee. Bowers, with split kings, promptly upped it to twenty. Purcell scratched his chin, shrugged, called. Cawthra said, "Hell with it," turned down his cards, stood up and went over to the bar.

Warren finished relighting his cigar, shook out the match flame, gave Bowers a broad smile. "Sure must think a lotta that king'a yours, Dale. Gotta 'nother one hid on me?"

Bowers eyed him levelly. "You want to play cards, or you want to gab?"

Warren's smile stayed in place. He picked a twenty from his stack, scaled it in, said, "Long's you put it that way, might's well boost her ten."

Dellacorte said, "Trouble with you bastards, you got no respect for money," and folded. Lee called. Bowers, teeth clenched, met the raise. Purcell hesitated, then called.

Lee resumed dealing. Bowers caught a seven, Purcell a queen, Warren a six, Lee the five of spades. Warren bet the limit. Lee, with two spades showing, raised. Bowers, aware that he was caught in the middle, decided he was now in too deep to quit and met the raise. Purcell called. Warren eyed Lee with mild interest—and reraised. Lee smiled, said, "That I didn't expect," and called, as did Bowers and Purcell.

The next round of open cards gave Bowers his second exposed king and a grunt of satisfaction; Purcell, a second open nine; Warren, a useless queen of hearts. Lee drew the three of spades to go with his four and five of the same suit: an apparent straight flush in the making.

"Kings bet," Lee said.

Bowers said, "Damned right they bet!" and dropped a ten into the pot with an exaggerated flourish. Purcell stared thoughtfully at his open nines, then called.

Warren raised the bet to twenty dollars.

21

Lee made it thirty.

There was a long pause. Bowers gulped down the rest of his drink, rubbed suddenly damp palms against his shirt front, said, "I say you're running a fucking bluff. Both of you."

"Your bet," Lee said quietly.

Bowers snatched two twenties from his stack, slammed them into the pot. "I'm raising! Whatta you think of that?"

Purcell said quietly, "Forty to me. Right?" and added two twenties to the mounting pile of currency.

Clark Warren drawled, "Don't see no reason to slow her down none," and reraised.

The others called. Lee lit a fresh Murad, then dealt each player a fourth exposed card.

Bowers had drawn the seven of clubs, giving him two pair—kings and sevens—on the board. Purcell now showed two nines and queen-ten; Warren, an ace, two sixes and a queen; Lee's eight of spades foreshadowed a straight flush.

Lee said quietly, "Up to you, Mr. Bowers."

The bank teller hesitated. He had his full house, kings high. Warren needed two more aces to top him; Lee's possible straight flush was a much bigger threat; Purcell, at best, was holding a smaller full house.

Bowers said thickly, "Ten's the bet," and tossed in two fives.

Amos Purcell calmly folded his hand.

Warren put down his cigar, eyed Lee's open cards. With the six of spades face down in his own hand, it would take a miracle the size of Lazarus rising for the young man to win the pot.

Warren made it twenty.

Lee made it thirty.

Bowers's face turned a vivid magenta. Warren reached for his cigar. Purcell and Cawthra sat unmoving. Frank Dellacorte stood up slowly and went over to the bar.

Bowers snarled, "Fuck it!", hurled his cards across the room, lunged to his feet, yanked his coat off the chair, and headed for the door.

Warren said, "Dale."

Bowers, his hand on the knob, looked back, scowling. Warren said, "Don't go runnin' off on us. This could git downright interestin'. . . . Doc? Mind fixin' Dale a drink?"

"Fix my own drink," Bowers snarled, and strode over to the bar.

Warren glanced at Lee, said, "Believe you raised me ten?" He snaked a twenty off his stack of bills, said, "Right back at you, Mr. Vance," and dropped it in.

Lee smiled and reraised.

Warren's cigar was out. He ground the stub into an ashtray with deliberate care, brushed his fingertips lightly together, leaned back in his chair. He said, "Seein' as how she's close to quittin' time anyhow, Mr. Vance, how 'bout I just put in, say, a hundred? And you call me? Git her over with? Now how's that sound to you?"

Lee smiled. "Whatever you say, Mr. Warren, is fine with me."

With the two hundred added to the pot, Lee dealt a card face down to the rancher, took one for himself.

Warren glanced at his hole cards. He said, " 'Fraid you gonna need that straight flush after all, Mr. Vance," and spread three sixes next to the one already open on the table.

Lee turned over three eights, dropped them alongside his fourth.

Warren said softly, "Well, I be damned." He stood up and hit the younger man a tremendous blow on the jaw, sending him and the chair crashing backward to the floor.

No one spoke. Lee's body jerked convulsively, then was still.

Elmer Cawthra set down his glass and knelt to examine

the man on the floor. Rising, he retrieved his drink, said, "Out cold. Got a little too slick with the deal, eh? Mite surprised none'a the rest of us caught on."

Bowers said, "I didn't take to the son of a bitch minute he walked in here. Should have known better'n to invite him, Doc."

"That last hand?" Warren said. "Started her off with a fake shuffle, crimped the deck for a shift cut. A peek here and there; dealt a flock of seconds. Them last two hole cards? Right offa the bottom'a the deck slick as calf shit."

"I sorta kept the corner of an eye on him all along," Amos Purcell said. "Never did catch on what he was up to."

Warren said, "Shame what pure greed can do to a man. Here he plays honest poker right up to the end—I'da known, he hadn't. Ahead six hundred easy. Good pay for a night's work? But no, he hasta go for a killin'."

Bowers was staring oddly at him. "How's it happen you know so much about card cheating, Clark?"

Warren grunted with mild amusement. "You figger I spent all my years singin' in the church choir?"

The man on the floor stirred, groaned faintly.

"Question right now," Frank Dellacorte said, "is what're we supposed to do about him."

"Gonna have to give that some thought," Warren said.

At seven-twelve that same morning, a black 1931 Essex sedan turned left off a dirt road bordering the Gulf of Mexico and pulled up behind a wide swath of towering red oaks.

Seated next to the driver, Anthony Malino stared through the windshield in stony silence. The man behind the wheel started to speak, then tightened his lips when he saw Malino's expression.

"Find out who they are," Malino said.

Douglas Wyeth thrust open the car door, stepped out, went

24

down the slight incline, walked over to the first body, and looked down at the face. The sightless eyes of Sal Calucci seemed to stare back at him. Bullets from a .45-caliber machine gun had ripped away the left side of his head at the hairline.

Within a radius of fifteen or twenty yards six more bodies lay sprawled on the narrow strip of sand and galleta grass bordering the gulf. Scattered about the area were three Thompson machine guns, a pair of sawed-off shotguns, and two Colt .45-caliber automatic pistols.

Wyeth moved impassively among the dead men, pausing only to make identifications. Finishing, he took a slow, sweeping look at the scene of the slaughter, then turned away, came back to the sedan.

"Three of our people, Mr. Malino," he said. "Calucci, Abbott, Bonara. The others I don't recall seeing before. No sign of Fannelli. It would seem he managed to escape."

Malino's face showed no expression. He said, "Cheech sold us out. Had to be him; other than me, nobody else knew when and where the load was coming in. Get in."

Once Wyeth was back behind the wheel, Malino said, "Find a phone and call the Turk. I want him down here fast with that boat of his. Tell him he'll need baling wire and cinder block, and to do the dumping at least a couple of miles off shore."

Wyeth started the motor. He said, "We really should get somebody out looking for that truck, Mr. Malino. Before . . ."

In a sudden burst of fury, Malino slammed a fist against the dashboard. "I don't *want* to know where that truck is! We got a fucking massacre here! This gets out and anybody ties me in with that load, I'll have every goddamn lawman and Prohibition agent this side of Washington, D. C. riding my ass! Now get me the hell away from here!"

5

A late model Hupmobile sedan, Dale Bowers at the wheel, coasted to a stop. Clark Warren opened a rear door, eased his bulk onto the shoulder of the narrow roadway. Bending, he looked into the back seat, said, "Outta there, boy!"

Lee Vance, not moving, stared at him coldly. "Then what? Beat me up?"

Warren said pleasantly, "Now why'd I wanta go do a fool thing like that, Mr. Vance?"

He reached in, closed a hand on the front of Lee's jacket, and with a single, smooth effort yanked him out of the car. Without releasing his grip, he said, "Y'all come back and see us real soon, hear?", then whirled the younger man around and slammed a boot squarely against his ass.

The powerful kick knocked Lee off his feet, sending him sprawling, face down, into a patch of stunted soapweed bordering the road. He lay there, half-conscious, fighting for breath. A brief silence, broken by two dull thudding sounds from somewhere close behind him. A car door slammed, a motor roared to life, tires whipped a whirlwind of dust into his face . . . and he was alone.

He stayed where he was, eyes closed, dimly aware that each breath was coating his lungs with reddish Texas dust.

. . . It was an unfamiliar sound. A dry clicking from close

by. Almost like dice being shaken briskly in a leather cup. Lee opened his eyes.

A rattlesnake.

A big bastard, coiled, ready to strike. Dark, with tan stripes forming a diamond pattern. Obsidian eyes, a darting twiglike tongue. And no more than three feet from his nose.

Sheer terror flooded Lee's mind. Mesmerized, unable to look away, he fought back an overpowering urge to urinate.

The clicking seemed to increase in tempo and volume.

"Shut your eyes," a silent voice said. "Don't move. Play dead, maybe it won't bite."

How can you close your eyes with a thing like that in your face?

"Shut 'em!"

He closed his eyes. Christ, this made it even worse! If that fucking thing jumped at him, he'd have no chance to dodge. He couldn't just . . . He had to open . . .

Seconds slipped by. Sweat soaked his shirt. The rattle slowed . . . stopped. A stirring in the grass. A slithering sound. Silence.

A bird twittered. He opened his eyes. No snake. Empty patch of grass but no snake. You sure? Somewhere behind him? Coiled, tongue flickering?

Let's say the snake *is* there. Way I hear it, a snake can't strike if it's not coiled. When it's coiled, it rattles. You don't hear it rattle, it's not coiled.

Okay. You're lying on your side. Now what you do is roll toward that empty patch of grass. Where the snake *had* been. Three quick rolls and before the damned thing can coil, let alone strike, you're up on your feet and away.

Nothing to it!

He tensed the muscles of his legs, shoulder, hips. Then with one tremendous burst of energy, he began rolling.

27

*   *   *

*T*hey had left the farm somewhat later than planned. By the time breakfast was over, the station wagon radiator filled from the well, and last night's blankets rolled and packed, six o'clock had come and gone.

Instead of using the coast highway, Ambrose had opted to take a back road that would bring him within a mile or so of Ben Proudfit's house on the outskirts of Corpus Christi. The Ford bounced along the narrow road's rutted surface at a steady thirty-five, and while the heavy overcast held no promise of rain, it kept the temperature and humidity at bearable levels.

Emily Dawson sat serenely in the back seat, hemmed in with bundles, darning a pair of Brose's socks ("Terrible hard on socks, that boy"), while Ruby half-dozed next to her husband.

The car rounded a sweeping curve. Ambrose straightened, said, "Somethin's up ahead there. Truck, looks like."

*T*he signs were wooden oblongs nailed to stakes set into the ground alongside the road and perhaps fifty feet apart. In turn they read:

IF YOUR RAZOR
ISN'T KEEN
TRY A BETTER
SHAVING CREAM
BURMA SHAVE

A lone cottonwood tree in full bloom stood a few feet beyond the last of the signs. Lee Vance stopped under it, set down his two suitcases—left by his late hosts—and got out his wallet. It contained two fives—and a scrawled note.

My dear Mr. Vance:

As chairman of the Corpus Christi office of the American Red Cross, please accept my personal thanks for your generous contribution of $1375 to our cause.

> Cordially,
> Dale Bowers

Lee said a few bitter words under his breath, dug into his watch pocket, found the lone fifty stowed there for just such emergencies. Stripping to the waist, he mopped himself dry with the shirt and undershirt, donned replacements from one of the bags, knotted a fresh necktie. A clothes brush got rid of most of the dust from his jacket and trousers. He buffed his shoes with the soiled shirt and undershirt, hesitated, sniffed at them, shrugged, and tossed both into the weeds. After combing his hair, he set the Panama at a jaunty angle, lit a Murad, upended one of the suitcases and sat down to wait.

No one would pass up a neat, well-dressed hitchhiker. Not in a state as neighborly as Texas.

6

The Diamond T truck's front bumper had ploughed into the guard rail of a wooden bridge spanning a narrow arroyo. Alfalfa bales stacked to the tarpaulin's hooped underside were visible above the closed tailgate.

The driver was nowhere in sight.

The station wagon coasted to a stop a few yards behind the truck. Ambrose shut off the engine, set the hand brake, left the car, and began walking toward the truck. "Hey!" he called out. "Anybody here?"

There was no response.

Ruby watched with mild interest as her husband circled the truck and disappeared. Emily finished a sock, reached for its twin. Then Ambrose reappeared near the front of the truck. "Hey, Ruby. C'mere a minute."

Ruby, annoyed at the prospect of getting out into the heat and dust, said sharply, "For what?"

"Just git over here, will you?"

She sighed, slapped open the car door, and joined him. "Whatta you want?"

He jerked a thumb toward the truck's cab. "Take a look."

Something in his voice alerted her. She stepped over to the window on the driver's side and peered in.

The body of Cheech Fannelli, his half-open eyes showing too much white, lay face up on the cab seat. Dark blood had

30

stained his shirt front and part of the floor mat. A clot of bluebottle flies was clustered around a gaping hole in his chest.

"Got hisself a loada buckshot, looks to me like," Ambrose said.

Ruby backed away from the window. "Makes me sick just lookin' at him. Anyhow, it's none'a our business."

"Not sayin' it is," Ambrose said. "But there's a man truckin' a load of alfalfa, ain't worth no more'n fifteen—twenty dollars, if that. And some sonabitch comes along and blows him to kingdom come? You gotta wonder why."

"Hitchhiker maybe," Ruby said.

Ambrose shook his head. "Sure doubt that. I never hearda no hitchhiker totin' 'round a shotgun."

"No use us standin' here talkin' about it," Ruby said. She turned away, started back to the station wagon, then stopped short, cocked her head, and sniffed at the air. She moved close to the truck. Bullets had left two holes just below the tarpaulin. Something wet and still glistening had stained the wood below them.

Ruby rubbed the wetness with a forefinger, sniffed at it as Ambrose moved up beside her. "What you got there, honey?"

She held the finger under his nose. He sniffed, looked up slowly, said, "Let's you and me take a look at what all's backa that alfalfa."

While Ambrose was lowering the truck's tailgate and tugging loose one of the alfalfa bales, Emily Dawson left the station wagon and joined him and Ruby. Ambrose pushed aside the bale, reached in, and brought to light a pyramid-shaped bundle, wrapped in burlap and coated with a residue of sea salt.

Using his jackknife, he slit the material and took out one of six brown short-necked quart bottles. An ornately decorated label read:

EDINBURGH HIGHLAND GLEN
PURE
MALT WHISKY
Bottled by:
L. G. Worth & Sons, Ltd.
Edinburgh, Scotland
Established in 1788

No one spoke. Ambrose, whose moderate use of alcohol over the years had been limited to bourbon and rye, pried out the cork, sniffed at the contents. He took a cautious sip, gagged, and spat it out.

Ruby stared at him. "What's the matter with it?"

"Nothin' at all," her husband said sarcastically. "Not if you got a likin' for cat piss, there ain't."

"Gimme that." She snatched the bottle and took a generous swallow of the liquor, then gave him a disdainful look. "Shows how much you know. This here's good Scotch whiskey. I used to know a fella drunk it all the time. And I tell you somethin' else, Brose. These days, this kinda stuff costs you a lotta money."

Ambrose said, "Not me, it don't." His shrug closed the subject. "Anyhow, the law's gonna hafta know 'bout what we run into here." He retrieved the bottle, recorked it, and tucked it back into the bundle. "Best we take this along. Case they go gittin' some idea we made it all up as a joke."

They returned to the station wagon. Ambrose stowed the burlap-wrapped package under a blanket roll and started the motor. Ruby, seated next to him, stared thoughtfully at the truck as the Ford squeezed past it and rattled across the bridge.

Suddenly Ruby grabbed her husband's arm. "Brose! Stop! Stop!"

Ambrose, startled, slammed on the brakes and the car

lurched to a halt, the motor stalling. He said, "What the hell's go—"

"We gotta go back."

"For what?"

Emily Dawson said mildly, "We come better'n twenty miles, girl."

Ruby's face had taken on a glow of excitement. "Not the farm. That truck. That whiskey! Git us a lotta money, we could up and sell it!"

Without waiting for a response, she plunged on. "There's this bootlegger used to come in the diner. Mr. Malino. Left a dollar tip even when he didn't have no more'n a cuppa coffee. I betcha we take it to him, he'd buy the whole shootin' match. Maybe git us three-four thousand, stuff that good!"

Ambrose's expression said she'd suddenly become the village idiot. Without a word, he started the car.

Ruby grabbed at the key, switched off the motor, and glared at him. "I wanta know why not?"

She got back an answering glare. "You had the sense God gave a jackass, you'd know why not. There's a law against it."

"Law? Don't make me laugh! Ain't nobody paid mind to Pro'bition far back's I can remember."

"They can stick you in jail, damn it! Just for havin' the stuff, let alone sellin' it. Now shut up about it!"

He reached for the ignition key. Ruby got to it first, snatched it away. "You listen to me, Ambrose Dawson! All we got to our name's thirty-seven dollars. How long you figger that's gonna last three people?"

"I don't need breakin' the law to make a livin'! Now gimme that damn key!"

"Law, law, law! What'd the law ever do for you? 'Cept take away your farm."

Those last few words hit home, rekindling his resentment

33

toward a system that, through no fault of his own, had stripped him—his family!—of everything.

. . . All right, say he did it. Sold that load of hooch to some bootlegger. Say . . . four thousand? Like Ruby said? That kind of money, he could pay off the bank, get his place back.

Ambrose took a slow, deep breath, shook his head. "Forget it, Ruby. Just ain't my waya doin' things."

In a sudden rush of fury, Ruby flung the key at him, shoved the door open, and jumped out. "Then I'll do it by myself!" she yelled. "And you can go straight to hell!"

Slamming the door, she whirled and set off at a run toward the truck, skirt and hair flying. Ambrose, his face contorted with anger, leaned out the window. "Git back here, damn it! *Ruby!*"

It was a waste of breath. Ambrose hesitated. Go after her, or risk calling what was more likely a bluff? The truck key was in the ignition and she was acting wild enough to go through with it.

In a matter-of-fact tone, Emily Dawson said, "The Lord moves in mysterious ways, son."

Ambrose turned his head sharply to look back at her. "Maw? Whatta you gittin' at?"

"Might be," she said placidly, "this is His waya reachin' out a helpin' hand to us, His children."

7

You are entering

SPLIT FORK

Pop. 1723
"The Pride of Texas"
P. J. Pruett, Mayor

*B*y seven that morning Split Fork's early risers were up and about. A black porter was sweeping the sidewalk in front of the Split Fork Trust and Savings Bank, the proprietor of the Bon Ton (ladies' wear) had finished raising the shop's blinds, and most of the stools at the Busy Bee diner (Tables for Ladies) were occupied. Fly-specked posters in the windows of a vacant store said the Tom Mix Circus would open at the county seat last April, three of the whittle-chaw-and-spit regulars were already sprawled on the bench in front of Oswald Tate's barber shop, Ketchum's drugstore sported a new window display: "Pebeco tooth paste keeps the Mouth Glands young."

The widow Belmont's rooming house was located over the Monroe hardware store two doors south of Main Street. In one of the cramped back bedrooms Virgil Lucas, wearing only a grimy pair of BVD's, lay spread-eagled and snoring on a narrow iron bedstead. An unpainted pine table held a battered alarm clock, a sack of Bull Durham, cigarette papers, an overflowing ashtray, a steel Jew's harp, and a tattered issue of *Captain Billy's Whiz Bang.* On the floor within easy reach, an uncapped mason jar contained a last inch of freshly distilled moonshine.

The clock's alarm had gone off at six sharp, then run completely down while Virgil snored on undisturbed. He was due at his job at seven-thirty, but as usual he would show up late.

*R*uby Dawson said, "What you gonna do, Brose?"

He looked at her woodenly. "What I gotta do. Long's I'm in this thing." He eyed the body of the late Cheech Fannelli. "But for sure this truck ain't goin' noplace less'n that dead fella's outta there."

He bent to reach into the cab, hesitated. Still time to back off, leave everything the way it was, and hunt up the sheriff. Go the other route and there'd be no backing off.

He looked along the empty road in both directions, then reached in, caught the body under the arms, dragged it out and over to the edge of the arroyo. Again he hesitated, then set his jaw, put the toe of a shoe against the side of the corpse, and shoved it over the edge.

Once he'd smoothed over the furrows left in the dust by the dead man's heels, Ambrose returned to the station wagon. He freed a shovel tied to one of the running boards, went back to the arroyo, and started down the steep slope.

Ruby slid into the front seat of the Ford and settled in to wait. Her heart racing with euphoria and excitement, her lips drawn into a strained rictus, she sat silently rehearsing what she'd say to Mr. Malino. About how we went and found this truck out there on the road with nobody around and all that whiskey in it. Only right off she'd just tell him 'bout it, make sure he'd pay a good price, then show him where the truck was so he could see for hisself what was in backa them alfalfa bales.

Four thousand wasn't near enough. She'd tell him five . . . *six!*

Emily Dawson said, "Car a'comin'. Sheriff, looks to me like."

The quiet words brought Ruby sharply back to reality. She thrust her head out the window and looked back as a dusty Chevrolet sedan showing the insignia of the Texas highway patrol coasted to a stop behind the station wagon.

Under the bridge, Fannelli's body at his feet, Ambrose had caught the sound of the approaching car. Clutching the shovel, he stood frozen, waiting for the vehicle to rattle across the overhead planks and continue down the road.

Instead, the motor died. Silence for a few seconds, then he heard car doors slam shut.

Ruby sat stiff with shock, nails digging into her palms, as two uniformed officers came up on opposite sides of the Ford. One walked casually over to the rear of the truck while the other stopped and peered in through the open window. He turned on an impersonal smile, said, "Mornin', ladies. Gotta problem here?"

Unable to force words through the tightness in her throat, Ruby could only shake her head.

"That truck, ma'am. Who's it belong to?"

Ruby swallowed convulsively, said, "My . . . husband."

By this time the second deputy was at the front of the truck. He glanced idly at the open window. Ruby fought to keep her eyes from flickering toward him. If he opened that cab door and so much as saw all that blood . . . .

The first deputy said, "Looks to me like she kinda run offa the road a little there, ma'am. How'd that happen?"

Suddenly Ruby's voice was back. In a spate of words, she said, "I guess so's it won't be in anybody's way, a car comes by. We up and lost the farm an' hafta go to Christi an' stay with kinfolk till my husband finds him some kinda job. Course, every'body outta work and all, I just don't know."

The second deputy was back. "Truck's okay, Tom. Banged up one'a the rail supports but not enough to matter none. Didn't see the driver nowheres around, though."

The first deputy gave Ruby a mildly puzzled glance. "Where's your husband at, ma'am?"

Ruby wet her lips, said, "Well, he . . . "

From the back seat, Emily Dawson said placidly, "My son's under the bridge answerin' a calla nature, young man. You was to wait, he'll be up direc'ly."

"Won't be necessary, ma'am." The deputy touched the brim of his hat in casual salute. "We'll be moving on. And good luck to you."

As the patrol car went by, the second deputy called out to Ruby, "Ma'am? That truck's left front tire sure needs some lookin' after. I was you I'd mention it to your husband."

Ambrose Dawson listened to the patrol car jounce across the loose planks over his head and fade into the distance. He picked up the shovel with an unsteady hand, forced a wry chuckle, then went back to preparing a final resting place for Cheech Fannelli.

8

*T*hus far, the only thing with wheels to show up was a decrepit Indian motorcycle with a lanky teenager in overalls at the helm. Lee's futile attempt to flag it down earned him his second ration of red dust for the day.

Not that he'd expected, or even wanted, a lift. A little information was all. Like where the hell he was and how far to the next town. Or at least where he could get four very large, very cold, very wet glasses of water. No question: He was in a tight spot. Down to sixty bucks and stuck out in the middle of nowhere.

Tight spots were not new to Lee. The only son of a wealthy Chicago contractor, his academic life at Northwestern University had ended abruptly when the school authorities learned he was peddling bootleg liquor and running a combination handbook and poker parlor—all for a select clientele from the student body.

During the next decade, Lee sold used cars in Cincinnati, abandoned that to push blue-sky stocks for a New York bucket shop. He served as a croupier in one of Arnold Rothstein's plushier gambling clubs before coming up with a foolproof way to knock down on the till, and was able to get out of town in time to stay healthy. In St. Louis he was into bootlegging on a small scale until a couple of East Side Sicilians came looking for him with heavy artillery.

Like any smooth operator, Lee knew the value of keeping up a front. To him, a clean collar and a fresh manicure were essential. His suits were tailor-made although not always paid for, he had most of the social graces, was equally at ease at a country club or the corner pool hall, and had once spent an exhausting weekend in a Baltimore hotel suite with Hollywood's Miss Clara Bow.

Once the motorcycle had disappeared, Lee returned to the shade of the cottonwood, plunked himself down on an up-turned suitcase, and propped his back against the tree bole. He thought of lighting a cigarette, but his dry throat talked him out of it.

Within a few minutes, lulled by the faint soughing of wind, the rustle of leaves and the voices of birds, Lee Vance was fast asleep. . . .

The distant sound of an approaching car awakened him. Vaguely disoriented, he remained where he was until the significance of that sound suddenly registered.

Springing to his feet, Lee scooped up his luggage and bolted for the road.

When the neatly dressed figure of a man suddenly showed up in the road some fifty yards ahead, Ambrose's foot never left the truck's accelerator. He wasn't about to pick up *any*body while hauling a cargo that could get his ass put behind bars. And even if it wasn't a lawman, it could be some boot-legger after what belonged to him. Looking to get back that load of cat piss, even if he had to shoot anyone in sight.

When the truck bearing down on him showed no signs of slowing, Lee dropped his bags and made a frantic dive for the roadside edge. For the third time within an hour he was engulfed in a cloud of dust, increased by a station wagon holding close to the truck's tailgate.

So much, he reflected ruefully, for the milk of human kindness, Texas style. He picked himself out of the weeds and was slapping dust from his pants when he heard a distant gunshot.

He glanced up in time to see the truck, now several hundred yards away, lurching wildly from side to side before finally swaying to a stop half off the road. It wasn't a gunshot after all, simply a blown tire.

Obviously a heaven-sent miracle.

*R*uby said, "Can you fix it, Brose?"

Ambrose stared glumly at the ragged crater in the truck's left front tire. "Don't rightly see how. Got a hole in there you can drive a goddamn heifer through."

His mother frowned at his use of the Lord's name in vain, but remained silent.

"I just hope," Ruby said, "too many'a them bottles didn't break. Way you was bouncin' them around."

Annoyed at the implied criticism, Ambrose snapped, "I wouldn't rightly know. Seein' as how I was tryin' to keep my neck from gettin' broke." He shrugged. "Might not matter, anyway. We don't find us a spare tire around here someplace, this buggy's gonna have to stay right where she sets."

Ruby stared at him, aghast. "Leave it? Just up and go? Why, you know we can't do that. It'd be . . . "

Her voice hardened. "You wanta leave it, don't you, Brose? Well, maybe you don't have no backbone, but *I* do. And I'm tellin' you right here and now that whiskey's goin' with us. Even if I gotta carry ever' last bottle on my back!"

Ambrose showed her a curled lip. "That so? Then you better start . . . "

"Good morning!"

The hitchhiker.

41

He had arrived unobserved. Ignoring the Dawsons' frozen expressions, Lee came over to join them at the truck. He let the two bags slip from his blistered fingers before slumping wearily against the tailgate.

"If," Lee said conversationally, "I had to die right now, I'd say drown me. In twenty feet of the coldest water this side of the North Pole."

Nobody laughed. Nobody even smiled. The Dawsons were eyeing him with a wooden politeness that didn't quite hide a thread of wariness. A wariness not just from fear he'd learn what was behind those alfalfa bales; there were more subtle reasons. His clothing, manner, and speech labeled him an outsider, certainly a Yankee, probably a Republican, possibly a Catholic or a Jew. But since the Dawsons were basically decent, normally hospitable, usually quick to aid anyone in trouble, they were incapable of telling this man to get the hell away from them.

Emily Dawson said, "Git the man a drinka water, Ruby."

Without a word, Ruby turned and moved toward the Ford.

Lee glanced down at the ruined tire. "It seems you folks could use some help, too. Where's your spare?"

Ambrose moved a shoulder, said, "Ain't so sure we even got one." At Lee's puzzled reaction, he added, "This here's a borrowed truck. Fella didn't mention 'bout no extra tire."

"One way to find out," Lee said. He squatted to peer under the truck bed for a moment; when he straightened, Ruby was back with a canvas-covered canteen. Lee uncapped it, drank deeply, handed it back along with a winning smile.

"Thank you, Miss . . . ?"

"Name's Dawson," Ruby said flatly. "*Missus* Dawson."

He gave her a second helping of his smile, said "Pleasure meeting you, Mrs. Dawson. I'm Lee Vance," then glanced at Ambrose. "The tire's under there. I'd say the tread's about gone but it should do for a while at least. Now let's see if we can come up with a lug wrench and the right size jack."

He turned and strode briskly to the truck's cab, jerked the door open, stepped onto the running board, leaned in, pulled aside the seat—and froze.

Nestled there, along with what he'd hoped to find, were a Thompson submachine gun and twin sawed-off shotguns.

A hand closed on his shoulder, yanked him out of the cab. He staggered back, managed to keep his feet—and was staring into the truncated muzzle of a shotgun leveled at his head.

Lee wet his lips, slowly lifted his hands. "You don't need that, Mr.—uh—Dawson. What you've got in there's none of my business."

Ambrose was as shaken as Lee. He knew damned well he couldn't just up and shoot the man. But let him walk away and he'd more'n likely go blabbing about some crazy farmer running around with a couple of sawed-offs and a machine-gun. The law got an earful of that, they'd be after his ass for sure!

He motioned for Lee to put down his hands, tossed the gun back into the cab, said, "You wanta know the truth, mister, we found this truck. Just settin' 'longside the road and nobody around. Minute I find out she's fulla all this whiskey . . . "

From behind him, Ruby wailed, "Brose!"

"—I figger to run her inta Christi and let the law worry about it."

A sixth sense nurtured by years of living by his wits told Lee he might have stumbled across something worth digging into. He said, "I know it's none of my business, Mr. Dawson, but even the thought of giving the police anything more than a two-for-a-nickel cigar bothers me. And of course you have to do what you think is right. I should remind you, though, that if there's a full load of whiskey on that truck, it has to be worth considerable money. Even if it's only moonshine."

"This ain't no moon," Ruby said sharply. "It's honest-to-God Scotch whiskey's what it is."

Ambrose was shaking his head. "Don't rightly matter anyhow. Seein' as how I got no sure waya sellin' the stuff."

Lee said quietly, "I might. Have a way to get it sold. If it *is* the real goods."

The Dawsons looked at him, expressionless, silent, waiting.

"Why," Lee said, "don't I take a look at it?"

*F*rom the Ford's back seat, Emily Dawson, wearing the same calm expression she'd one day be buried with, handed her son the blanket-wrapped bundle. He moved to the front of the car, set the packet gingerly on the hood, then gestured to Lee. "There she is."

Lee unfolded the blanket, lifted out the burlap sack and removed the bottle Ambrose had opened earlier. He glanced at the label, kept his expression neutral, and eased out the cork. He sniffed at the contents, took a sip, let it rest on his tongue for a few seconds, then swallowed.

Ruby said, "I was right, huh? Real good Scotch?"

Lee recorked the bottle, rewrapped it, put it down. He said, "Any idea how many burlocks are in that load?"

At Ambrose's blank look, Lee said patiently, "You wrap six bottles in burlap, shrink it tight in salt water to keep them from banging together and breaking. Bootleggers call them burlocks. Now how many would you say?"

"Best I could make out," Ambrose said, "she's packed solid. Front to back, roof to floor. Gotta be a good . . . five—maybe six—hundreda whatever it was you called 'em."

"Making it," Lee said, "better than three thousand quarts."

Ruby said, "How much money you figger we can git for it?"

Lee said, "We're not talking about a load of turnips you

peddle on some street corner, Mrs. Dawson. What you need is a connection. Somebody with a bankroll, someone in the rackets." He paused, then added, "Someone who won't rob you blind and dump you both in an alley with your throats cut."

Ruby's avid expression lost some of its edge. She said, "Well, there's this here big bootlegger. In Christi. Real nice fella name'a Malino, only they call him Tony Large. We was thinkin' he might buy it offa us."

"Okay," Lee said. "You go to him. He looks at what you've got, says, 'Fine. How much do you want for it?' What do you tell him?"

Ruby looked uncertainly at her husband: no help there. "We was thinkin' . . . mebbe three-four thousand?"

Lee managed to repress a sardonic smile. "Four thousand dollars. I see. Did it occur to either of you that this might have been Malino's whiskey? *Before* it was hijacked? And you can be damned sure it was a hijack—one that went wrong for some reason—or it wouldn't have been left sitting out here.

"So you bring it to Malino, tell him how you happened to find it. He gives you a pat on the back, slips you a few bucks for your trouble. Fine. You're home free. With a fat wallet.

"But," Lee continued, "let's say it wasn't Malino's truck at all, that it belonged to some other outfit. And they get the idea *you* hijacked it. *For* Malino."

He shrugged, spread his hands. "Mr. Dawson, you wouldn't live long enough to get yourself a decent haircut."

He gave them time for the words to sink in, then reached into the blanket, brought out one of the bottles and held it up.

"Edinburgh Highland Glen," he said with slow emphasis. "They don't come any better. Even before Prohibition it went for around eleven dollars a quart. But these days? Any boot-

45

legger knows his onions can cut this five ways and still have his customers lining up to fork over ten bucks a fifth for it."

Ruby, face shining, earlier doubts gone, was drinking in every gold-plated word, while her husband showed only a politely skeptical expression.

Lee said, "Let's say there's three thousand quarts, okay? Now I'll tell you something. Get that load to the right place and we'd be paid on the spot. At least fifty thousand dollars. And it could go as high as sixty."

Those last three words seemed to hang in the air between them. Ambrose took a deep, unsteady breath, said, "Mister, you have got to be the biggest damn liar I ever come across. Ain't nobody gonna up and pay me that kinda money, don't matter for what."

Lee said, "You're wrong, Mr. Dawson. The right man would pay it. And I know the right man."

Not until then did it first dawn on Ambrose that this Yankee was in dead earnest. He was aware of a surge of excitement—and with it a leavening of suspicion. He said, "Say I was to believe ya. Whatta *you* figger to git from it?"

"One third," Lee said.

To Ruby—already seeing herself behind the wheel of a Pierce-Arrow, wrapped in mink and tossing dollar tips to hairdressers—his words were like a kick in the shins.

"A third!?" she yelped. "That's . . . that's . . . "

"Somewhere around twenty thousand," Lee said evenly.

"For doin' what, I'd like to know."

"For getting you forty thousand, Mrs. Dawson. If you remember, you were ready to take a lot less before I came along."

Ambrose, annoyed, said, "Man's got a right to set his price, Ruby. What's got into you?"

She turned to glare at him. "We got us a chance to git rich, that's what's got into me. 'Steada givin' it to some—some *drifter*."

In the seething silence, a car door slammed and Emily Dawson joined them. She gave Lee a probing hairline-to-shoes look, said, "Name's Mrs. Em'ly Dawson, young man. Seems about time somebody 'round here interduces us."

Lee's smile was both winning and respectful. "Lee Vance, Mrs. Dawson. Nice meeting you."

"I been listenin' to all this talk," Emily said bluntly. "Kinda hard doin' business with a man we don't know the first thing about."

Lee looked her straight in the eye. "If you need references, Mrs. Dawson, I'm afraid I can't furnish any. But I've never killed anyone, and you won't find my picture tacked up in the post office. The best I can do is assure you I know what I'm talking about." He spread his hands, shrugged. "And . . . ask you to trust me in this."

Emily Dawson's expression didn't change. "Ain't yet heard you say where we hafta go to git us all this money."

"Kansas City."

That shook them. Even Emily blinked. Ambrose said, "Don't see how we could do it, Mr. Vance. We ain't got the means to go travelin' no 'leven—twelve hunnerd miles."

"Be closer to fourteen hundred," Lee told him flatly. "Most of it back roads, a lot of circling around, no night driving.

"Why? Because one slip and some peace officer or one of Uncle Sam's booze hounds will want to know what's behind those alfalfa bales. Every minute, every mile, we'll be walking a tightrope.

"Only maybe you'd rather not hear that kind of talk. Maybe you'd rather hear how the trip will be a breeze, a nice little outing, with picnic baskets and candles on the birthday cake. Well, you won't hear it from me. It'll be a long, tough haul, we'll need all the brains and nerve and luck we can put to-gether—and we could still end up in jail."

He paused, saw the unwavering determination in

47

Ruby's eyes, the doubt in Ambrose's expression, the firm thrust of Emily's chin.

"But you know something, folks?" he said. "We'd be prize saps not to give it a whirl."

"Thing is," Ambrose told his mother, "we first gotta swing past Christi, drop you and Ruby off and give Ben some kinda excuse why I'm gonna be goin' on."

Ruby said, "Nobody said nothin' 'bout me stayin' behind."

"Well, I'm sayin' it now," her husband said sharply. "Me and Mr. Vance here's gonna have enough to look after 'thout a couple'a women too."

"Is that so? You listen here, Ambrose Dawson! I was takin' care'a myself long 'fore you showed up and I don't need . . ."

Ambrose slammed a fist against his thigh. "Maw, will ya talk some sense inta her?"

"Seems to me," Emily said quietly, "Mr. Vance oughta have some say in this."

Lee said, "I understand your son's concern, Mrs. Dawson. But since neither of you ladies seems the nervous type, and since bootleggers don't usually take their families along on business trips, it could keep people from getting nosy."

9

*I*t was an hour short of sundown when they drove into Mule
Bend, Texas, population 617. It stood astride an unpaved
main street made up of a combined general store and post
office, a feed-and-grain store, a poolhall, Dottie's Diner, a
blacksmith shop-cum-filling station, Lou's barber shop, a
bank, and the First Baptist Church.

Both vehicles pulled into the service station and stopped
on either side of the single pump. As Ambrose and Lee
stepped from the truck's cab, an elderly, tobacco-chewing
attendant in grease-stained overalls and a leather apron sauntered over.

"He'p you fellas?"

"Gas 'em both up," Ambrose said. "And while you're at
it, might see to the radiators."

Emily left the Ford and, with a ladylike lack of haste,
headed for the station privy. Ruby slipped from behind the
wheel, said, "Couple things I need at that store, Brose."

Lee said, "I'll tag along. If you don't mind."

Ambrose, frowning absently, watched them cross the road.
They moved past a dust-covered Chevrolet touring car and
a horse and buggy, cautiously circled a huge tumbleweed
nesting near the grocery doorway, and went in.

The interior was narrow, deep, cluttered, and smelled
mildly of pickle brine. Wall posters pitched the virtues of

49

Mail Pouch and Star chewing tobaccos, Campbell soups, Barbasol shaving cream, Camay and Pears soaps. A five-year-old girl stood frozen in front of a display case of penny candies. At the rear three old-timers were grouped over a board game set up on a barrel top.

Ruby went directly to the long counter and waited her turn while the proprietor, middle-aged and overweight, measured out four yards of oilcloth for a young woman in from the farm.

An ice chest stood at the far end of the counter. Lee fished out two dripping Coca-Cola bottles, used an opener tied to the chest, and offered one to Ruby. "Go ahead," he told her. "Flush out some of your Texas dust."

She gave him a darting, narrow-eyed glance tinged with suspicion, hesitated, then, without a word, took the bottle and turned away.

Still sore, Lee decided, at the idea of his winding up with a third of that sixty grand. Well, the lady had one hell of a shock coming to her. . . .

He moved over to a wide table piled high with work clothes and idly began sorting through them.

At the counter, the clerk said, "Be somethin' else for you, Miz Jessup?"

"No sirree," Mrs. Jessup said emphatically. "Spent too much already. Way money is these days."

The man bagged her purchases, penciled in the total on the page of a ledger from under the counter, and unfroze the five-year-old with a licorice "turtle" from the candy case.

Once mother and daughter were out the door, the clerk smiled warmly at Ruby. "Evenin', ma'am. Don't believe I seen you 'round these parts before."

"Just passin' through," Ruby said curtly.

The smile flicked off. "What can I do for you?"

Ruby, her cheeks pinking, pointed to a stack of sanitary

50

napkin boxes, camouflaged by plain brown-paper wrappings, on the shelf behind him. "One'a them."

Lee, carrying an armload of clothing, paused as one of the Monopoly players landed on a railroad. Lee said gravely, "I were you, I'd buy it, sir. Man can't own too many railroads."

Three graying heads came up and Lee was looked at out of steady eyes set in blank faces. He said apologetically, "Just trying to help," and moved on to a table stocked with field-hand straw hats.

Ruby paid her bill and the clerk was bagging the three items when Lee, one of the hats tilted rakishly on his head, came up to the counter. He spread out two pairs of Levis, two work shirts and three pairs of cotton socks.

He grinned at Ruby, pointed at the hat. "How do I look?"

"Like some kinda play actor," she sniffed.

His smile undented, he said, "A girl *did* tell me once I looked like Wally Reid." He turned to the clerk. "Carry any cigarettes?"

"No tailor-made ones, no sir. Not much call for 'em. I can sell you the makin's, though."

"Wouldn't know what to do with them," Lee admitted. "How much do I owe you?"

"Well, let's see now." The clerk wetted the pencil tip and began writing down figures while fingering through the pile of clothing. " 'Mounts to eleven dollars, thirty-five cents. Includin' them two drinks you took."

Lee brought out his wallet, removed the two fives, then shrugged and glanced at Ruby. "Care to make a small loan, Mrs. Dawson? Say . . . two dollars?"

Ruby stared at him, aghast. "That all the money you got?"

"Hate to admit it," he said cheerfully. "But like Mr. Hoover keeps saying, prosperity's just around the corner."

"Well, of all the nerve! Just how you figgerin' on . . ."

She stopped short, suddenly aware that the clerk and the

three Monopoly players had become a fascinated audience. She fumbled open her handbag, snatched out two singles, and threw them on the counter. Lee added his two fives. About to hand him the change, the clerk hesitated, then placed it on the wood between them. Ruby was reaching for the coins when she caught Lee's faintly mocking smile. She grabbed her bag of purchases and, shoulders squared, stalked over to the door and out.

Lee scooped up the change, gave the clerk a broad wink, picked up his bundle, and trailed after her.

She was standing at the curb waiting for him, her temper hanging from a frayed thread. "One thing I wanta know, mister smart aleck. How we supposed to git all the way to Kansas City on a measly thirty-two dollars and sixty cents? Tell me that."

He eyed her with open disbelief. "Thirty bucks? The three of you?"

"You heard me. All your big talk and you can't even pay your own way. And why you went and got all them clothes, I'd sure like to know."

He frowned, annoyed. "You expect me to go batting around the country in that truck wearing a hundred-and-sixty-dollar suit?"

Her breath snagged at the sheer gall of this Yankee. "Well, ain't—that—just—too—damn—*bad!* Next time you git hungry, try eatin' a pair'a them *pants!*"

An impatient voice yelled, "Hey, Ruby!"

They turned. Ambrose stood glowering at them from in front of the service station. "Git over here, will you? Man wants his money."

She muttered an indelicate word and left Lee standing there.

The elderly attendant was recapping the Ford's radiator and Emily Dawson was back in her accustomed place when Ruby arrived.

Ambrose, sounding irritated, said, "Pay the man."

"Comes to four-seventy," the attendant said.

Her lips clamped into a thin line, Ruby once more dug into her handbag, snapped a five from the meager fold of currency, slapped it into the man's hand, and got back three dimes from a pocket of the leather apron.

As Lee joined the group, the attendant glanced over at Ambrose. "Let'cha have a good buy on truck tars, mister. You sure could use . . . "

Ruby chopped him off in mid-sentence. "Got all the tires we need, thank you."

Lee said, "Which tires and how much?"

Ruby said, "You don't catch me payin' for no tires."

Both men ignored her. "Well, lessee now," the attendant said. "Happens I just got in these Goodyears, run you nine-fifty apiece. Two of 'em oughta take care'a the truck. Now that right back tar on the Ford sure looks like she's 'bout to let go any minute. Run you five bucks." His lips moved silently, adding it up. "Comes out twenty-four for the three. An' a'course I'd be puttin' 'em on for you, free'a charge."

Lee said, "Can you break a fifty?"

Ruby's jaw sagged . . . snapped shut.

Sensing the tension between the two, the attendant said, "Don't see why not," and hurried off toward the garage before Lee could be talked into changing his mind.

Her voice deadly calm, Ruby said, "You got fifty dollars, why'd you go borrow them two dollars from me?"

With forced patience, Lee said, "You'll get your deuce back, Mrs. Dawson. And don't get the idea I like shelling out my own cash. But considering what's on the truck, what I'd like a hell of a lot less is a blowout in the middle of the sovereign state of Texas."

The man in the leather apron reappeared, wheeling a heavy-duty jack and a dolly loaded with three tires. He said, "No offense, mister, but mind payin' up front on these?"

Lee fished out the fifty-dollar bill, handed it over, got back a twenty and six singles from a pocket of the apron. "I do thank you, mister. Like I said, no offense meant."

"None taken," Lee said pleasantly.

Ambrose said, "That diner you got over there. How's the food?"

"Best you ever et," the garageman said. A sudden grin bared tobacco-stained dental plates. "I'd up and marry Dottie myself, my old lady'd stand still for it."

Ambrose said, "Tell you what you do, Ruby. Long's we gotta wait around, you and Maw and Mr. Vance here go get some supper. Fetch me back a san'wich or somethin'."

Before Ruby could object to this new threat to their assets, Lee said, "My treat, Mrs. Dawson?"

She saw the mockery in his eyes and angrily turned her back.

Once the others had left, Ambrose moved over to watch while the garageman positioned the jack under the truck's front axle. The man said, "Looksa them springs, mister, you sure got yourself a lotta alfalfa in there."

The observation was one Ambrose had been prepared to answer from the first. "Got us a loada furniture in backa them bales," he said. He smiled, then added, "Not to mention the parlor stove."

The man gave him a sidelong glance and a knowing grin. "Beat the bank to it, huh?"

" 'Bout the size of it," Ambrose said.

With the jack in place, the garageman was reaching for the ratchet handle when Ambrose said, "There some place 'round here we can put up the truck and car overnight 'thout makin' anybody mad at us?"

The man nodded. "Big field over backa the Baptist church. Reverend Mather talked the town into puttin' up a couple'a privies and pipin' in runnin' water so's a fella can wash up.

Fact a lotta towns doin' that nowadays, what with the hard times an' folks goin' broke and headin' out west and all."

It suddenly dawned on Ambrose that this damned old fart was talking about *him*. Ambrose Dawson. Just one more poor bastard couldn't take care of his own family. Well, he'd by God turn *that* around! Get his farm back minute he laid paws on that booze money. Then go ahead and fix the place up like he'd been meaning to do all along. . . .

The garageman said, "Way the reverend puts it, he'pin' others in their hour'a need's the Christian thing to do."

He reached for a lug wrench and went to work.

10

*I*t was well after dark on the second day when the two ve-hicles crossed a rickety bridge spanning a small creek, pulled off the narrow dirt road, and drew up behind a stand of loblolly pines.

While Ruby and Emily were whipping up sandwiches cut from the ham butt and dishing out saucers of peach preserves, the two men pored over a battered state map Lee had talked the Mule Bend blacksmith into parting with.

The city slicker had been replaced by a good ole boy in denims, a dark gray cotton shirt, and yellow heavy-duty work shoes picked up before leaving Mule Bend. Now, freshly shaved, hair neatly combed, he was seated on the truck's running board, smoking a Murad and watching Ambrose move a finger along a winding line marking their route.

The finger slowed to a stop. "Puts us about here," Ambrose said, tapping the map. "Forty-fifty miles this side'a Split Fork."

Lee said, "How much of a town is it?"

" 'Bout a couple thousand," Ambrose said. "Corn and hog country, I hear. Ain't been there myself."

"Supper's ready," Emily Dawson called out.

They dined under the brilliant rays of a full moon, the women seated on the station wagon's running board, Lee and Ambrose across from them on an alfalfa bale.

"Twenty-one hunnerd and seventy-two dollars," Ambrose

was saying. "I says to the man, 'Mr. Willis,' I says, 'where in the billy-blue hell am I supposed to git that kinda money on such short notice? And he says, 'Wisht I could tell you that, Mr. Dawson, but you know well as I do what the Republican Party's done to this country last three years. Way things are,' he says, 'the bank's lucky if she can stay open much longer.' "

He put down his sandwich, gulped water from one of the canteens. "Well, I wasn't hardly more'n back home when they up and foreclosed on us. Hunnerd and sixty'a the best damn acres this enda Texas. Grow prit' near anything you set your mind to."

It was all coming out in a relaxed, conversational tone, without bitterness, without self-pity. He paused to take another bite of his sandwich, said, "Anyhow, Mr. Vance, case you been wonderin', that's how come I throwed in with you on this whiskey business. Made my mind up to git me back my farm—even if I gotta be a bootlegger to swing it."

Lee smiled. "If we can make it to Kansas City, Mr. Dawson, you can afford half a dozen farms."

"Providin'," Ruby said flatly, "nobody steals our money 'fore we can git hold'a it."

Because she had put into words an underlying uneasiness shared by Ambrose and his mother, they maintained a blank-faced silence.

Lee said quietly, "You don't know that much about me, Mrs. Dawson."

Ruby had blurted out the words impulsively. But having gone this far, she was not about to back down. Making no effort to mask her contempt, she said, "Don't go thinkin' I been stuck on a farm all my life. I seen a million fellas like you. Not ten cents in their pocket, never done a day's work in their life, always lookin' for a ride on the gravy train. I never yet run into one yet wouldn't steal pennies off of a two-year-old!"

Intentionally or not, she had succeeded in putting Lee firmly on the spot. He couldn't let the attack pass unchallenged—not if he hoped to hold the respect of these hicks. And without that respect he could lose their trust—something he couldn't afford to lose. Not at this stage. . . .

He finished the last of his sandwich, reached for the peach preserves. Ignoring Ruby, he said, "I don't know why it is, Mr. Dawson, but it seems any time a chance to make a killing shows up, there's always some half-assed know-it-all around ready to gum up the works."

His voice took on an edge. "Well, the lady's your wife. So tell her to shut her mouth and keep it shut—or as far as I'm concerned you can run that load of booze into a ditch and go back and live off your relatives."

Ambrose eyed him levelly. "Mr. Vance," he drawled, "You'n me, we made us a deal. I ain't heard nothin' so far likely to make me back out on it."

His expression took on a chill cast. "But if Ruby's right, and you try cheatin' me outta what's rightfully mine, they won't be no place on God's green footstool you can hide."

With supper out of the way, separate but equal bathroom areas were selected, Sears, Roebuck catalogue pages were substituted for more conventional toilet paper, and quick dips into the cold creek water flushed away two days of sweat and dust.

Once Ruby and Emily were bedded down for the night in the station wagon, Ambrose rolled and lit a cigarette, boosted himself up next to Lee on the truck's tailgate, said, "Still figger we gonna pull this thing off, Mr. Vance?"

Lee, heavy-eyed with exhaustion, shrugged. "No reason why not. Long as we stay inconspicuous. That and a ton or two of luck." He watched Ambrose take a deep drag on his cigarette. "Those things hard to put together?"

The other man grinned. "Wouldn't say so. All she takes to find out is a little time and a lotta wasted tobacco. Run outta them tailor-mades, huh?"

"Finished my last one after dinner."

"Might come across some, we git to Split Fork." Ambrose got out his sack of Bull Durham and the folder of rice paper. "Here, lemme roll you one."

Twelve seconds later, he handed over a smooth cylinder of tobacco and offered a light. Lee drew in a lungful of the acrid smoke, winced, exhaled, nodded his thanks.

They went on sitting there in companionable silence for several minutes before Ambrose pinched out his cigarette and slid to the ground. "Time to hit the hay," he said. "We git goin' 'round six."

He walked away, heading for a night's sleep in the truck cab. Lee pried off the heavy work shoes, peeled away his socks, growled a few blistering words to match the newborn blister on his left heel. He piled two blankets on the tailgate as a mattress and crawled under a third.

He lay there, bone-weary, muscles aching, hands cradling the back of his head, and looked up at the big bright stars of a Texas night.

"There must be an easier way," he muttered wryly, "to make a dishonest living."

He toppled into sleep.

Over the years, unpleasant things had happened to the face in the mirror: a puckered scar bordering the left ear, the splay-tipped nose broken in a barracks brawl, two missing lower canines, and at the moment, four fresh nicks left by a straight razor in an unsteady hand.

Virgil Lucas was thirty-three, tall, rawboned, slope-shoul-dered, with close-set eyes, stick-out ears, and coarse black hair receding at the temples. The son of a Harlan, Kentucky, coal miner, he had enlisted in the army at nineteen, saw two years of action in the big war, came out physically unscathed, and was handed an honorable discharge on his twenty-second birthday.

However, army life had left Virgil with a drinking problem—one that at times plunged him into brief but wildly hallucinatory episodes.

During the next twelve years, he drifted from job to job, strictly a loner with no goals beyond the bottle, an occasional woman, and enough ham and eggs to keep up his drinking strength.

Now, in the grip of a mammoth hangover, Virgil stuck bits of toilet paper to the razor nicks and ran a broken-toothed comb through his hair. Leaving the bathroom, he retraced a wavering path along the hall to his room, sank onto the edge of the unmade bed, and on the third try was able to roll and light a cigarette. He would have given his scarred soul for a proper drink, but during the night what was left of the jar of white lightnin' had somehow evaporated.

He butted the cigarette, resisted the urge to crawl back under the covers, and fought his way into an oil-stained pair of tan coveralls, mismatched socks and cracked leather work shoes. After listening at the door to make sure the widow Belmont wasn't on the prowl (he was in no shape to bear up under another of her temperance lectures), he headed for the stairs and began inching his way down the steps.

The time was 8:17 A.M. Virgil was now forty-seven minutes late for work.

*T*hey had been underway for an hour or so when the Diamond T turned on them.

A short burst of metallic popping sounds under the hood was followed by a harsh pounding. Ambrose, behind the wheel, slammed in the clutch, cut off the motor, and eased the truck to a stop. He was out of the cab and had his head under the open hood by the time Lee joined him.

"How bad is it?"

Ambrose stepped back, straightened. "Sounds to me like a fuckin' connectin' rod tore loose."

"Can you fix it?"

"Need the right tools first. And even if I had 'em, I wouldn't know no more where to start than a piss ant."

By this time the station wagon had pulled up behind the truck. Ruby hurried over to them. "What's the matter, Brose?"

Her husband glared at her. "You wanta know what's the matter? I'll tell you what's the matter. It's the enda the goddamn line, *that's* what's the matter!"

Lee said quietly, "Hold up a minute, Brose. You sure the truck can't make it to Split Fork?"

He got back a humorless snort. "You're talkin' a good twenty-five, thirty miles. Try it and you got yourself a pile'a junk for an engine inside'a five."

"Okay," Lee said. "We can't get the truck to Split Fork, we get Split Fork to the truck."

They stared at him blankly. "What I'll do," he said patiently, "is drive the Ford in, find a mechanic—place that size must have at least one—and bring him back here."

"Run you a lotta money," Ambrose said.

"There's a way around that. The town should be big enough for me to flush out a discerning Scotch drinker or two who can afford the best. So, I take along a few bottles, peddle them for enough to foot the repair bill. Might even end up with some left over."

"Be takin' one hell of a chance," Ambrose warned, "you git aholda the wrong fella."

Lee smiled. "Trust me," he said.

61

11

As he reached the street, blazing sunlight hit him like a mailed fist. He raised a shaking hand to shield his eyes, turned his back, collided with a corner of the building, and hung there while a wave of nausea slowly subsided. Cautiously he opened his eyes. A cardboard poster tacked to the wall at nose level said sharply, INSIST ON GROVE'S CHILL TONIC.

Virgil pushed himself erect and moved off along the restless sidewalk. Twice he sidled carefully around invisible objects. A passerby's cheerful "How ya doin' there, Virgil?" went unheard. A passing car kicked up a choking cloud of dust along the unpaved street.

It was 8:24 when he entered the Busy Bee cafe.

At this late hour only five of the stools at the long wooden counter were taken. Elmo Sykes, owner of a General Motors dealership, was having flapjacks and bacon at one of the six window tables. An early version of the jukebox, mercifully silent, stood at the far end of the room.

Virgil found an isolated stool at the end of the counter and gingerly climbed aboard. The middle-aged waitress said, "Mornin', Virgil," plunked a cup of coffee in front of him, added a cracked plate holding two squares of cornbread, called out, "Scramble two, bacon easy," and moved away.

Using both hands to cradle the cup, Virgil lifted it to his lips, took a cautious sip, set it gently down. The fingers were steadier now, his vision clearer. The effects of another in the long history of Virgil's "mornings-after" were beginning to fade.

The door banged open and a brawny young man sauntered in. He was decked out in doeskin pants, fringed Hollywood-cowboy shirt, two-toned knit vest, and a white Stetson flaunting a braided silver band. He swept the room with an insolent glance, flopped down at one of the tables, lifted polished leather boots to the other chair and yelled, "Hey, Blanche. Rustle me upa cuppa java and a hunka that gooseberry pie."

Blanche, juggling three loaded plates, ignored him. He snapped, "Hey, c'mon! I ain't got all day," slammed his feet to the floor, and swaggered over to the record player.

A blast of country music tore through the room. Virgil's hand jerked, spilling half his coffee. He took a deep breath, carefully set down the cup. He stood up, put a hand against the counter to steady himself, then moved to the rear wall, bent, and yanked the cord out of its socket.

The music died on a long, whining note. The young man came off his chair, eyes blazing, hands balled into fists, and stepped in front of Virgil. "What'n hell ya think you doin', mister? Stick that fuckin' cord back where she was or it's your ass, hear?"

Virgil reached into a pocket, brought out a nickel, tossed it onto the table, turned, and moved off toward the vacated stool. The young man hesitated, took two tentative steps after him, stopped.

A customer snickered.

The young man snatched up the coin, flung it across the room, and stalked out.

Virgil's order was ready and waiting. While Blanche refilled his cup, he picked up his fork and started on the eggs.

*R*uby said, "Guess you been wonderin' why I wanted a ride in with you."

Lee, behind the wheel, glanced at her. She was sitting stiffly erect, expressionless, clasped hands resting in her lap, eyes looking straight ahead.

"No," Lee said. "Not really."

Ruby hadn't slept well the night before. For the first time since the trip began, her thoughts had been on what lay ahead for her when this was over. All that money—and all Brose could talk about was gettin' back his farm! How about her? He ever think of askin' her what she wanted? Or was she just supposed to shut up and go back to feedin' the chickens, sloppin' the hogs, scrubbin' his dirty clothes? Instead of maybe go do some travelin' around, see somethin' 'sides the ass-end of a cow.

It sure needed some thinkin' on. . . .

She turned her head slowly to look at him. "Well, I guess I had no call sayin' them things last night, and I just thought I'd say so. That's all."

"The part," Lee said, "about my stealing pennies from two-year-olds." He shook his head in mock reproach. "Not nice of you."

"Well, I'm sorry if you're sorry."

"What've *I* got to be sorry about?"

"Callin' me half-assed. Fronta my own husban'."

He glanced down at the modest swell of her hips. "I still say you don't miss it by much."

"How'd you like a swift kick in your you-know-whats?"

Suddenly they both were laughing. Briefly, softly, but the tension between them from the first had eased—at least for the moment. Ruby fumbled through her black, Sunday-best pocketbook, brought out a sack of Bull Durham and a folder of papers. "Want one?"

Lee lifted an eyebrow. "Didn't know you smoked."

"Brose don't like me to, but I sneak one in when he ain't lookin'."

"You make it, I'll smoke it."

"Pull over a minute."

*T*hey rode in silence for another mile or so. Ruby put out her cigarette, settled back in the seat, glanced at the man beside her. "Where'bouts do you live?" she said, then added hastily, "If you don't mind me askin'."

He looked over at her, grinning. "As of right now I'm up to two addresses—a 'twenty-nine Ford station wagon and a big old Diamond T truck."

"You don't wanta tell me, then don't."

"If you're asking where I was born and raised: Chicago."

"No wonder," she said tartly, "you know so much about bootleggin'."

"Lot more goes on in Chicago than bootlegging and one-way rides, Mrs. Dawson. Matter of fact, Cleveland was where I ran into my first honest-to-god mobster. Skinny little Hebe, with a mouthful of gold teeth and a perpetual hard-on. Sorry," he added hastily.

He eased the car past a dip in the road. "That was a big year for me," he said, smiling wryly. "I'd just turned twenty, owned the town's finest collection of pawn tickets, got booted out of college, and was flat broke. My old man handed me a hundred bucks and said, 'My son, if I should ever lay eyes on you again in this life, I'll personally kick your ass over the Wrigley Building.' "

He laughed, shook his head in ungrudging tribute. "He could've done it, too. Probably still can. Even though he's nearly sixty, worth a couple million bucks, and hasn't laid a brick or picked up a sack of cement as far back as I can remember."

Ruby eyed him with mingled disbelief and resentment. She said evenly, "I think you're a big liar, that's what I think.

65

Anybody's got two million dollars, they ain't out hitchhikin' around in the middle'a nowheres."

"I didn't say *I* had it."

"Said your paw did. You went back, you'd git it."

"I wouldn't touch it, Ruby," he said quietly. "Not for anything. Now or ever."

Her expression told him she believed *that* the way she believed in purple leprechauns.

"Don't misunderstand me," he said. "I'm as fond of money as the next guy. I just want to get it my way. Have a little . . . well, fun—excitement—while I'm at it."

Ruby's lips flattened into a thin line. She said contemptuously, "You think lookin' for money's some kinda play game? Like maybe huntin' for Easter eggs or somethin'?"

"I wouldn't put it that way. I'm only saying . . ."

"You shoulda been my maw's kid. You wouldn'ta got no hunnerd bucks offa her. She run a crummy rooming house, and I didn't git hardly no schoolin' 'cause she was too damn lazy to make beds and scrub floors and empty out the slop jars."

Lee, eyes on the road ahead, put up a calming hand. "Hey, look. I'm sorry if I . . ."

She wasn't listening. "I wasn't even yet thirteen when she found me with halfa my clothes tore off and this old man tryin' to git me on the bed and his pecker in me. You wanta know what she done about it? She got so damn mad at him she up and raised his room rent five dollars a month!"

She took two deep breaths, sank back in the seat, said, "I don't know about you. But soon's me and Brose git holda that whiskey money, we gonna do us some real livin'. 'Fore I end up in a rockin' chair with a face fulla wrinkles and my teeth in a glassa water!"

Lee let a few moments pass, then said mildly, "Aren't you forgetting something, Ruby?"

"Like what?"

"You heard him last night. That money's supposed to get the farm out of hock. Which puts you right back feeding the chickens and milking the cows."

His words brought into sharp focus Ruby's splintered thoughts from the night before. Didn't she have as much right to that money as Brose did? Hadn't been for her, he'da gone off and left that booze settin' back there where they found it. Well, if he thought for one goddamn minute she was gonna give in, just go back to livin' on that farm—then he had hisself another think comin'!

A road sign spelled out SPLIT FORKS CITY LIMITS.

The moment Virgil came into the lot, Fred Barsch, a native Iowan and present owner of the Split Fork Garage (Prompt Service at Fair Prices our Specialty) stormed out of the office to confront him.

"Goddamn it," he roared, "where the hell've you been? You were supposed to be working on Joe Gifford's brakes two hours ago."

Breakfast and the passage of time had brought Virgil reasonably close to normal. He gestured apologetically. "I'm gonna git right on it, Mr. Barsch. Got up feelin' kinda poorly, I guess you'd call it, but I'm . . . "

" 'Poorly', my ass! Come dragging in here late four days in a row, you drunken bastard! For two cents, I'd . . . "

Virgil hit him.

The blow caught Barsch squarely in the left eye. He staggered back, barely managed to keep his feet, then sprang at the mechanic, flailing at him with both fists. A roundhouse swing landed flush on Virgil's chin, sending him sprawling. He jerked his head aside barely in time to avoid being kicked in the face, came catlike to his feet, and tore into the garage owner with an avalanche of short, hard punches.

The larger man retreated, tried to cover up, caught a solid

right to the mouth, and reeled back. Virgil charged, swung wildly, fell, then threw a shoulder against Barsch's legs, nearly upsetting him.

A crowd made up largely of silent men and barking dogs parted reluctantly as a grossly fat man in dungarees, a shiny, oversized star pinned to the pocket of his khaki shirt, shoved his way through. He stepped between the two arm-weary gladiators and clamped a ham-sized hand on Virgil's shoulder. (You don't grab hold of the local Rotary Club president and a fellow member of the I.O.O.F.)

"Nothin' more to see, folks," he told the crowd. "Now y'all git on 'bout your business, hear?"

Nobody moved. Sheriff Traub glanced over at the winded garage owner, said, "Might be a good idea, the three of us was to go in your office, Fred? Kinda git this thing talked out?"

Unnoticed, the Dawsons' station wagon had drawn up across the street.

"Like hell we will," Barsch snarled. "I fired this man for constantly coming in late, and he attacked me. Now you get the son of a bitch out of . . ."

"Call me that again, mister big man," Virgil said softly, "I gonna make you hard to find."

Traub said mildly, "Now you hush up, Virgil, 'fore I go hurtin' my knee on your nuts." He turned to Barsch. "Man got wages comin'?"

"Three days. You going to let him get away with this, Andy? I mean this business of him attacking me?"

Traub shrugged. "Might git him ninety days for assault. Case you was a mind to press charges and all."

"I might just do that. Teach this . . . this man a lesson. Meantime, I'll get him his fifteen dollars."

He turned and walked toward the garage office. The crowd had begun to drift away. Virgil said, "You fixin' to jug me, Sheriff?"

Traub eyed him coldly. "Son, you shamed a prominent man. In front of a lotta folks known him a good twenty years."

"He hadn'ta foul-mouthed me, I wouldn'ta swang on him."

Traub shook his head. "Virgil, I can bear a fool and I've been known to git along with drunks. But when a man's both, he's plain beyond my patience. You got any belongin's here?"

"Got me my tools."

"Go round 'em up while I git you your money. Then you by God pick a road outta this town. While you're still healthy and as close to sober as you're ever gonna git."

*F*rom the front seat of the station wagon, Lee and Ruby watched the mechanic, lugging a heavy tool bag, leave the garage area, move off along the sidewalk, and disappear around the next corner.

Lee started the motor, said, "As a bookie friend of mine used to say, 'Brains is nice, but luck's what makes you rich,' " and pulled away from the curb.

Virgil had stopped to let a momentary wave of dizziness pass when the station wagon drew up alongside him.

"Talk to you a minute?" Lee said through the open window.

Virgil eyed him blankly, then picked up the tool bag, came slowly over to the car, and looked in.

Lee said, "We saw what happened back there. Makes it tough, losing a job these days."

Virgil blinked at him, waiting.

"We've got this Diamond T," Lee said. "Been giving us a bit of trouble. I can pay you a few bucks to fix it."

At the moment, money was far down Virgil's priority list. He said, "I do thank you, mister. 'Cept I ain't feelin' so good. Right now, I couldn't fix ya a hoe handle."

Hangovers are easy to diagnose. Lee reached over the seat back, pushed aside the folds of a blanket-wrapped bundle on the floorboards. "Maybe this would help," he said blandly. "Least it's recommended for snakebite."

The mechanic stared down at the exposed bottles. The tip of a pale tongue appeared, circled suddenly dry lips. "Where's this trucka yours at?" he said hoarsely.

*F*rom beneath the Diamond T came the sounds of metal against metal as a wrench tightened the bolts supporting an oil pan.

Ruby, in the front seat of the station wagon, watched her husband and Lee standing off to one side, deep in a low-voiced discussion. Finally Ambrose gestured, nodded in agreement, and turned away.

A few moments later, Virgil reappeared, dragging his tool bag after him. He stood up and was wiping his hands on a grease-stained rag when Lee came over. "Well, how about it?"

"Had a loose bearing cap," the mechanic said. "Guy worked on it last never cinched her up tight. Shoulda had his ass kicked for him."

"Then it's okay?"

"You mean is she gonna run; yeah, she'll run. How *far* she'll run, that's somethin' else again."

"How about Kansas City?"

"Mister, what with all that weight you got on there, *and* the shape that motor's in, you gonna be stoppin' at a lot of garridges 'fore you git far's Kaycee. That I garantee ya."

"Virgil," Lee said, "how'd you like to make yourself five hundred dollars?"

The mechanic eyed him levelly. "You *got* five hundred dollars?"

"It'll be waiting for you. In Kansas City. All you have to do to earn it is keep the wheels turning on both these cars till we get there."

70

"Well . . . I don't know 'bout that. Long way to . . ."

"Five hundred dollars," Lee said. "Plus a quart of that Scotch every other day."

The sign said, THE SPLIT FORK EMPORIUM, GLADYS DUSH-ALL, PROP. Lee pushed open one of the double doors and went in.

The wide, deep room appeared to be stocked with every item known to man. Racks of clothing covered two walls, a third had boxes of shoes stacked to the ceiling, overloaded grocery shelves lined the center aisles, an entire section was devoted to hardware.

And not a customer in the place.

A rail-thin elderly woman with steel gray hair and youthful eyes stood by the cash register at the near end of a long wooden counter. In a surprisingly deep voice, she said, "Somethin' I can do for you, young man?"

Lee said, "Do you carry cigarettes? Tailor-mades?"

She stared at him in total disbelief. "If that don't beat all! Business ain't bad enough already, you gotta march in here lookin' for the one blessed thing I *don't* have!"

Lee showed her a conciliatory smile. "I'm sorry, ma'am. Maybe you'd know who might?"

"I don't, nobody does. Sell you the makin's?"

"Afraid not." Lee turned away. "Thanks just the same."

He was halfway to the front door when the woman called out imperiously, "Young man! Git back here!"

Lee obeyed. It didn't occur to him not to. The woman said, "You stand right there till I git back. Hear me?"

"Yes, ma'am."

She strode briskly down one of the aisles, disappeared. Several minutes passed, then she reappeared, came striding toward him carrying a small paper sack. She dropped it on the counter in front of him.

"Cost you a dollar," she said.

Lee opened the bag and dumped four packs of cigarettes on the polished wood.

"Musta been back there better'n a year," the woman told him. "Used to order 'em in special for old Doc Fuller till he up and died on me. Them was left over."

Lee eyed the packs doubtfully. "Sackett De-Nicotined? Never heard of them."

"You come in here wantin' tailor-mades. Them's tailor-mades. Be a dollar."

Lee paid her.

Oklahoma

—◆X◆—

June 1932

12

*T*wenty-two hours after leaving Split Fork they crossed the Oklahoma state line, then veered left at a fork in the narrow, bumpy road to take a less grueling route. Shortly before nightfall, with nothing yet visible except open prairie, the two vehicles passed a roadside sign that read:

City Limits
HARGROVE, OKLAHOMA
Pop. 4619
Campgrounds 2 miles
One night only!

The grounds proved to be more than a simple camping area. Located a quarter-mile from a railroad right-of-way, they were set in a grassy expanse dotted with lofty elms and fitted out with toilet facilities, two primitive bath houses, and a number of iron cooking grills mounted on bricks. Three earlier arrivals, lares and penates tied to the sides and tops of their cars, had already taken up residence for the night.

While Ambrose prowled the railroad tracks in search of stray lumps of coal, Emily and Ruby took hasty cold-water baths. By the time Lee was bathed, shaved, and into a clean shirt, Ambrose had made use of his coal harvest to feed a cooking fire.

They dined sumptuously on grilled ham steaks, mashed potatoes and gravy, with hot cherry preserves as dessert.

Virgil was the first to finish. He thanked Emily Dawson politely and wandered off. Lee polished off his portion of preserves, sighed contentedly, and put aside the dish.

"My compliments, Mrs. Dawson," he told Emily. "Can't remember having a more enjoyable dinner."

"What with all that drivin' and fresh air," Emily said modestly, "man's bound to be hungry 'nough to eat most anything gits set in fronta him."

Lee lit one of his Sackett De-Nicotined cigarettes, then held out the pack to Ambrose. The farmer gave it a wary eye, shook his head, and set about rolling his own.

Emily said, "Might you be a Jewish person, Mr. Vance?"

"For chrissake, Maw!" her son said sharply. "That any your business?"

Emily, unabashed, said, "Now, Brose. We just settin' here visitin'. And I'll thank you not to go takin' the name'a Our Savior in vain."

Virgil had perched himself on the truck's lowered tailgate out of their view. He set aside a half-empty bottle of whiskey and picked up the Jew's harp. After a moment's reflection he made his decision, and the soft strains of "Sleepy Time Gal" took over.

Back at the fire, Lee said, "No, Mrs. Dawson, I'm not Jewish." He smiled. "Although come to think of it, I do have this aunt who goes in for Christian Science."

It was a feeble joke at best, but Emily took it at face value. "My, now isn't that interestin'!" she said. "Why, they had this Science church in the town next to us. Mrs. Wallford was real active in it."

She looked over at Ambrose. "You remember Mrs. Wallford, Brose. Her and her husband came out to the farm on a Sunday once, stayed over for supper?"

76

Ambrose, sounding annoyed, said, "Can't say's I do."

"Had this harelip, poor soul," Emily told Lee. "Made it terrible hard to git at what she was sayin'. She got started in on how rewardin' I might find the Science church, was I to join up. I listened real polite for a time and fin'ly I says to her, 'Mrs. Wallford,' I says, 'I was born a Baptist and I was christened a Baptist by complete and total emmersion in the waters of Calhoun Crick, Columbia County, Arkansas. On topa that,' I says, 'my dear daddy was a deacon of the Baptist church till the very day he passed to his reward.'

" 'So you can see,' I says to her, 'it's kinda late for me tryin' to git into Heaven by the back door.' "

She settled back triumphantly. "Well sir, Mr. Vance, I just wish you coulda seen her face! You never *heard* a woman so full of apologizin'. Said right out she hadn't any thoughta tamperin' with my faith, and how there's room in the Lord's house'a many mansions for them as truly loves Him, don't matter a whole lot how they go about it. Then I ask her does that hold for the heathen Chinese and all them Papists a-bowin' down in fronta graven images. Well, that poor woman! I tell you, Mr. Vance, she was sure up a stump! Just didn't know *what* to say!"

Ambrose said grumpily, "She'da been a Baptist, she'da knowed what to say. And woulda, too."

Emily gave him a full helping of glacial eye, snapped, "Like the Good Book says, 'Mock not, lest ye be mocked!' "

Ambrose made a half-amused, half apologetic gesture and began putting together another cigarette. Lee said, "Odd you mentioning Columbia County, Arkansas, Mrs. Dawson. I ran into a fellow here a few months back who came from there. A jockey. Named . . . Colby, I think it was."

"Can't say I recollect the name," Emily said. "Not su'prisin', seein' as I left from there the same day I was wed to Matthew Luke Dawson and went off to homestead in Texas."

"The farm you just lost?"

Emily nodded briskly. "Be forty-four years this comin' month. All we had startin' out was a span'a mules and three heada horses. The good Lord gave me the strength to work the fields and butcher the hogs 'fore I was more'n seventeen yearsa age."

Ambrose drawled, "Ain't like that any more, huh, Maw?" He gave Ruby a sidelong glance. "Nowadays girls just naturally git everything handed to 'em on a gold plate."

His wife's lips snapped into an angry line. "Don't git so smart! How'd you like bein' a girl settin' pins in a bowlin' alley 'fore you was yet fifteen? How'd you like standin' on your two feet all day and halfa the night for nothin' more'n tips and meals? Or mebbe havin' a buncha truck drivers a-grabbin' your backside till you couldn't set down on it?"

It wasn't easy but Ambrose managed to keep a straight face. "Sure hate findin' out I liked that last part."

Ruby's voice turned shrill. "Mebbe you think I liked it better gittin' up five in the mornin', and feedin' chickens and huntin' aigs and wadin' 'round in cow shit! Well, you . . . "

Emily said sharply, "Ruby. I don't care to hear that kinda talk."

"Then tell him to leave me alone. So mebbe I didn't butcher no hogs or shoot me no Mexicans when I . . . "

Emily stiffened, suddenly furious. "Ruby! You hush your mouth! Hear?"

No one spoke. The only sounds were the shrill skirl of cicadas and, faintly, a loose version of "Washboard Blues" on Virgil's Jew's harp.

Lee had tried to cover his startled reaction to Ruby's last few words, but not before the older woman's sharp eyes had caught it.

After an awkward pause, Emily said quietly, "A sad thing it was, Mr. Vance. And way I look on it, nothin' for me to take pride in. Came about the first spring Luke and me was on the farm. There was these two Mexico men come up from over the border. Way they'd do way back then. Lookin' to steal and to burn, and women they could *de*file."

Her words slowed, stopped. She stared down at her folded hands, then raised her eyes and went on, her voice steady. "Luke was away. Gittin' one'a the mares bred if I recollect right, and I just happen to look out the kitchen winda, and here they come, sneakin' up, guns ready. Well, Mr. Vance, I was bad scared I tell you! I up and grabbed Luke's repeatin' rifle from where it was kept and let loose at them two men with the whole load.

"Well, here 'long 'bout sundown Luke gits back and there I am—out behind the barn a'shovelin' and a'prayin'. Prayin' as much for my own soul as for them two."

She spread her hands. "Took a long while 'fore I was to git over it. Many's the night I laid there in my bed, seein' them misguided creatures a'bleedin' out their lives in the dust."

Lee said awkwardly, "It was a brave thing to do, Mrs. Dawson."

She looked at him with the stern majesty of a Biblical prophet. "A long while back, Mr. Vance, the good Lord in His infinite wisdom said to His children, 'Thou shalt not steal.' Way I look at it, I was servin' as His instrument in keepin' them thievin' Mexicans from breakin' His holy law."

She got to her feet and began gathering up the plates. " 'Steada settin' 'round gabbin'," she said briskly, "I better rid up these here dishes and git myself to bed."

A hand closed firmly on Virgil Lucas's ankle and tugged, jarring him awake. "Wha—wha'cha doin'?"

"Keep your voice down!"

Virgil, bleary eyed, peered at the face bent over him. He mumbled, "That you, Mr. Vance?"

Lee straightened, stepped back. "Something I want you to do for me."

With a second effort, the mechanic managed to get to his feet. "Sure, Mr. Vance," he said fuzzily.

The reek of whiskey fumes pushed Lee back an extra step. He handed Virgil four flat metal objects. "Those are Oklahoma license plates. Use them to replace the ones on the truck and the Ford."

Virgil stared at him, slack-jawed. "Wha' for? Somethin' the matter with what's on 'em now?"

"No," Lee said. "But I don't want some limb of the law asking why anybody'd bother hauling a two-bit load of South Texas alfalfa clear across the state of Oklahoma."

Virgil shrugged. "If that's what you want. Git right on it come sunup."

"It can't wait till then," Lee said firmly. "Not with all these strangers around here. They see you switching plates, somebody's likely to wonder why. Out loud. And that, my friend, we can't afford—not with what's riding on that truck."

Virgil made a resigned gesture and started to turn away when something occurred to him. "Lemme ask you somethin', Mr. Vance. These here plates. Mind sayin' where you got 'em at?"

"From where," Lee said patiently, "they won't be missed. Good night, Virgil."

13

*R*uby suddenly clutched her stomach, cried out, and bent double.

Ambrose gave her a startled glance. " 'S'matter with you?" Ruby groaned again, began to gag. From the back seat, Emily Dawson said sharply, "Pull over!"

Ambrose swung the station wagon off the road. By the time it skidded to a stop, his wife had the door open and was vomiting violently onto the ground. Emily left the back seat, jerked open the driver's door, snapped, "Git out, Brose."

She slid in, put soothing hands on the younger woman's shoulders, holding her till the shuddering convulsions had subsided, then pushed her gently onto her back across the wide seat.

Lee left the truck cab, joined Ambrose. "What happened?"

"Ruby's sick. Been pukin' her guts out." He turned, raised his voice. "Maw? How's she doin'?"

No answer. Emily was prodding the girl's abdomen with stiffened fingers. Ambrose came over to the open window. "C'mon, Maw. She gonna be okay?"

Emily smoothed back Ruby's hair, patted her shoulder reassuringly. She looked up, saw her son's concerned expression. She said, "For sure, it ain't her appendix actin' up on her. Not likely somethin' she et else we'd all be down with it. Now you go find two–three blankets and git 'em spread out on that grass over there. And long's you're at it, dig out one'a them goose-down pillas."

Once they'd managed to get Ruby, still in pain, bedded down behind a row of sumac bushes well off the road, Emily said, "How far we from the next town?"

Ambrose said, "That'd be Mumford. I'd hafta say mebbe ten miles."

"Then you git in that car and you hightail it up there. Find you a drugstore and tell 'em—now you listen to me, Brose— you tell 'em you want two bottlesa Lydia Pinkham's Vegetable Compound." She repeated the name with slow emphasis. "Figger you can remember that?"

"Maw, for Godsake!"

"Git goin' and git back. Poor girl's suffered enough as it is."

City Limits
MUMFORD, OKLAHOMA
Pop. 1474
Home of Mohawk Leather Co.
Est. 1907

Ambrose parked the station wagon in front of the Mohawk County State Bank two doors from the entrance to Gorman & Green, Drugs and Notions. As he reached the bank, the door flew open and two young men wearing pin-striped suits and gray fedoras charged out waving handguns. One, carrying a bulging pillowcase, collided with Ambrose, sending them both sprawling and jarring the gun loose. It hit the cement, fired once, and bounced into the gutter. The bank robber made a frantic dive for the weapon, but Ambrose got to it first.

As his hand closed around the butt, the world blew up.

*   *   *

"Close enough," Lee Vance said. "Pull in back of those trees."

Virgil waited till two cars passed from the opposite direction, then steered the truck over a few bumps, stopped behind a row of cottonwoods, and switched off the headlights.

Lee said, "Listen to me, Virgil. You sit right where you are till I get back. And no drinking, you hear me? Not—one—damn—*drop!* Understood?"

Virgil, cut to the quick, said stiffly, "You got no call to go yellin' on me, Mr. Vance. I can git along 'thout it."

Lee gave him a conciliatory pat on the knee. "Sorry. Ambrose missing like this has me wound up tighter than a dollar watch."

He opened the cab door, stepped out, and showed Virgil a twisted smile. "Pray for me," he said and disappeared into the night.

Virgil leaned back, rolled a cigarette, got it burning, then reached under the seat and brought out a half-empty bottle.

"Couple snorts," he muttered, "never hurt nobody."

*H*e was in his early fifties, with smooth, unweathered skin and a full head of iron gray hair. His thin white cotton jacket hung open, revealing a striped dress shirt with a plaid bow tie nesting high against a prominent Adam's apple.

"I'm Doctor Jensen," he said. "How are you feeling?"

Ambrose Dawson wet his lips. He was aware of lying on a narrow bed with a lumpy mattress, of being jaybird naked, of being covered with a thin blanket, of having the worst goddamn headache in the history of mankind. He said, "Feel like shit, tell you the truth. Head's 'bout to kill me."

"Not at all surprising," Jensen said. "Good thing Mrs. Miller's a slight woman or you might well have ended up in Joe Ligget's funeral parlor. Do you recall any of what went on out there?"

Ambrose fought to bring fractured images together. "Two . . . fellas. One of 'em bumped into me. . . . Yeah! Damned if he didn't up and take a shot at me!" He shook his head, winced. "That's 'bout the size'a it, Doc."

"From what we can figure out," Doctor Jensen said, "you seized the gun, took a shot at one of two men and kept him from getting away with better than seven thousand of the bank's money. He's now behind bars. But it seems Martha Miller mistook you for a robber and hit you over the head. With what, nobody seems sure of."

He drew up a chair and sat down next to the bed. "At the moment, you're in one of the three so-called hospital rooms Mumford can brag about. Mrs. Jensen and I live on the floor below."

Ambrose was barely listening. He had to get out of here, get hold of that . . . what the hell was it now—pink something?—and get back to the truck. He said, "Sure do 'preciate all you done for me, Doc. Now if you'll git me my clothes, I'll up and light outta here."

"I can't advise that," Jensen said. "You took a severe blow to the head, resulting in a mild concussion. Let's see how you are come morning. And I'll have your clothes for you then; Mrs. Jensen felt they could stand washing after what you went through.

"Besides, Henry Mumford aims to offer you a reward for saving the bank's cash." He smiled. "Knowing Henry, it'll be a modest one, I'm sure. Right now, I want you to get a good night's sleep, see how that headache of yours is by morning."

He stood up. "Something else. There'll be a couple of state troopers showing up around noon. Evidently they want to find out if you can furnish some description of the man who got away. Goodnight."

84

He switched off the overhead light and went out, closing the door behind him.

Ambrose lay in a cold sweat. One thing for damn sure, he wasn't waiting around for no state lawmen and a bunch of questions. Not with what was on that truck! Bare-assed or not, he was getting out of here.

He pushed aside the blanket, sat up, cautiously swung his feet to the floor. The pounding in his head seemed to worsen, but he could bear that. He stood up gingerly. The room tilted, dipped sharply—and he was back on the bed.

*T*he station wagon was alongside the curb a few doors from a drugstore still open at this rather late hour. Three men were standing in front of the bank, deep in a low-voiced conversation.

Lee entered the drugstore. A slim, small-boned young clerk in a white coat and sporting a barely visible blond moustache came out from behind a minuscule soda fountain.

"What'll it be, mister?"

"A friend of mine," Lee said, "was in earlier today. To pick up a couple of bottles of something called Lydia Pinkham's Compound. Did he get them?"

"Couldn'ta," the clerk said. "Been out of it more'n a week now."

"But he *was* in?"

"Not less'n it was afore noon, he wasn't. I been on since then."

Lee stood lost in thought. It had been well into the afternoon when Ambrose drove off for Mumford. No question he'd made it; the Ford was parked down the block. . . .

The clerk said, "Guess you missed out on all the goin' ons, huh?"

Lee glanced up sharply. "What goings on?"

"Bank stickup," the clerk said, relishing it. "Two fellas.

Didn't get nothin' though. One'a the crooks got nabbed when this other fella jumped in. Ended up he got *his*self shot. Real big hero, this other fella. Kept them robbers from gittin' away with alla the bank's money."

"He have a name? This hero?"

The clerk scratched an ear. "All I heard, he's some outta town fella."

"You said he was shot. How bad?"

"Damn if I know. Have to ask Doc Jensen 'bout that."

"Where do I find him? This doctor."

"Turn right at the next street, go down 'nother block or so. Big white house, got hospital rooms upstairs. You figger he's this friend'a yourn? This fella?"

"That," Lee said grimly, "could be."

Ambrose was ready to make a second try. He closed his eyes, got to his feet in a series of small moves. The drumbeat in his head had faded to a dull throbbing. He took a slow step. The room lurched . . . steadied. The only light came from the unshaded window, the only sound faint music from a distant radio or victrola.

He took three sliding steps toward the door . . . stopped. Say he did make it to the street, how far'd he think he'd get running around buck naked? To the car? Hell, he didn't even know how to find where at he'd left it.

Ambrose returned to the bed, stripped away the blanket, wrapped himself in it toga fashion, then wobbled over to the door. He opened it slightly, peered out. Light from a dim overhead bulb showed a stretch of narrow hallway with a sharp turn at the rear. The music from the floor below had been replaced by voices from a radio program he recognized: "Just Plain Bill."

Front stairs? Too risky. Gotta be back ones somewhere.

He eased the door open, stepped out, and began tiptoeing down the hall, aware of the coarse nap of the carpeting under his bare feet.

He reached the bisecting corridor. Dark as the devil's hip pocket. He stepped hesitantly into it.

A hand shot out of the blackness, clamped fingers across his mouth. A voice whispered, "Easy! It's me!"

Ambrose clawed the hand loose, snarled, "Christ a'mighty! You like to scared the shit outta me!"

"Not so loud!"

For a moment neither man moved or spoke. Then Lee said, "I was told you got shot."

" 'Nother fella. Tried robbin' the bank."

"I suppose you know they're calling you a hero?"

"Yah. Got me a reward comin'. And a couple'a the state law boys s'posed to show up around noon wantin' to ask me questions. How long we gonna hang 'round here chinnin'?"

"You can't go running around like that. Where are your clothes?"

"Where I can't get at 'em, that's where."

"There's a back door. Follow me down, wait just outside till I can bring the car around to the side street. I'll give a couple of short beeps on the horn as soon as I can get there."

"Best make it fast. Afore this sawbones shows up wantin' to tuck me in for the night."

"Ready?"

"Uh-huh."

Lee led the way to a steep flight of steps going down. At the bottom, a few feet of narrow hallway ended at a door opening onto a small porch with a wooden icebox in one corner.

"Wait here," Lee whispered. "And when you hear that horn, take off!"

Two wooden porch steps brought him to the ground. He

hesitated, gave the area a sweeping glance. Windows in nearby homes were dark. Good. People in small towns. They go to bed early, they get up early, they lead dull lives. Right now he could use a bit of dull life himself.

He slipped through the shadows cast by two giant poplars, eased open a gate in the white picket fence. No one in sight. He stepped out, turned left and sauntered along the sidewalk. Just a local boy, wearing overalls and a straw hat, big old work shoes on his feet, on his way home from the pool hall.

He turned left onto the main street and walked on till he reached the drugstore. It was still open. He passed it, continued on to where Ambrose had left the station wagon.

It was gone.

The young clerk with the almost moustache was turning off the drugstore lights when Lee came in.

"My friend's station wagon," he said, biting off the words. "Parked near the bank. Maybe you can tell me what the hell happened to it."

The clerk lifted a blond eyebrow. "Not there?"

"Not there."

The clerk rubbed a thumb thoughtfully against his chin. "Well, now . . . he leave the keys in it?"

"Probably."

"Then I'd hafta guess Elwood took her in."

"And who," Lee said between clenched teeth, "is Elwood?"

"Sheriff. Tom Elwood. He don't like cars bein' left out on the street all night. Could get stole."

"Where do I find him?"

"Jail house. Turn left, go down two blocks, turn right 'nother block. Can't miss her. Better get a move on, though. Tom goes home 'bout this time'a night."

*I*t was a low rambling wooden building. Behind an open window a tall, lean, middle-aged man in uniform sat behind a desk, feet up, smoking a cigar.

Lee stood in the shadows of a huge oak across the street. He could make out the lines of the station wagon in the deep shadows at one side of the building.

Now what? Go over there, barge in, give the man a big smile? Understand you picked up my friend's car. Doc Jensen says he's well enough to leave, so if you'll just let me have the car keys I'll take care of the rest.

No. That wouldn't do it. Ambrose was supposed to talk to the state cops around noon. Besides, he had this reward coming to him from the bank. Man's a fucking hero, remember?

All he could do was wait. Wait till the guy called it a day and went home. Wait and hope the key had been left in the ignition. Wait while Ambrose stood back there on that porch sucking wind, scared to stay and too scared to leave.

The minutes limped by. Lee stepped behind the oak tree and lit a cigarette, shielding the match flame from view of any chance passerby. He finished it, swore under his breath, lit another . . .

The man behind the desk leisurely ground out the cigar butt, lowered his feet to the floor, yawned hugely, and got out of the chair. He closed the window, scooped a ring of keys from the desk top and left the room. Taking a last look, Lee decided, to make sure the would-be robber hadn't tunneled his way out.

The sheriff was back. He tossed the keys into a desk drawer, locked it with a key from his pocket, switched off the desk lamp, and disappeared.

Lee dropped his cigarette, stepped on it. The station's front door opened and the uniformed man came out. He turned a key in the lock, made sure the door was secured, and moved off into the night with a loose, easy stride as Lee edged deeper into the tree's shadow.

He gave it another two minutes, let an open-bed truck rattle by, then strolled across the street and into the macadamized parking area flanking the station.

The Ford wagon was waiting for him. He tried the door. Unlocked. He slid in, fumbled in the darkness for the ignition slot.

No key.

Lee hammered his fist against the steering wheel. The sheriff must have it locked in that desk of his. Hot-wire it? He hadn't the foggiest idea how to go about it.

The glove box!

He yanked back the lid, struck a match and pawed through a welter of junk. No key. He slammed the lid shut, sank back in the seat. What next? Break into the jail office, dig through desk drawers?

The floor mat!

Kneeling in the cramped space, he struck a match, peeled back the square of rubber. Gleaming in the flickering light was a short length of shiny metal.

With its headlights off, he turned the station wagon into the street adjoining Mumford's self-styled hospital and coasted to a stop from where he could make out the rear porch. No parked cars, no lighted windows, no one out for a stroll.

And no sign of Ambrose.

Lee shrugged, gave the horn two quick taps. Ambrose sprang from somewhere near the porch and raced toward the car, naked legs flashing, blanket flapping wildly. He tripped, was up like a cat, vaulted the picket fence, plunged through the open car door and into the back seat.

"Welcome home, hero," Lee said, and stepped on the gas.

*T*hey eyed the limp, snoring hulk slumped behind the wheel of the truck.

"We better git us to K. C. in a hurry," Ambrose said. "Afore this soak ends up drinkin' the whole load."

"Had to expect it," Lee said philosophically. "Least he had enough sense left not to go wandering off."

They managed to move Virgil's dead weight next to the window on the passenger side of the cab. Ambrose squeezed in behind the wheel while Lee took over the station wagon.

With both vehicles back on the road, they set out for where Emily and Ruby would be tearing at their hair with worry.

*T*hey found them behind the sumac bushes, huddled together under blankets and sound asleep. It seemed that Ruby, even without Lydia Pinkham's help, was back to normal. Whatever had ailed the girl, Emily put the blame on the rigors of travel. The fact that it was also the wrong time of the month for her was delicately passed over.

14

Shortly before sundown they drove through Grossmont City, Oklahoma, population 3288. A few blocks farther on, a battered brown canvas tent large enough to shelter a congregation of two hundred took up most of an empty lot flanked on either side by wide bands of trees and bushes. An enormous cloth banner above the entrance flaps read:

One Week Only
Come One—Come All!
CHURCH OF THE TRUE FAITH
Tonight's Sermon
"What Does Jesus Think of *You?*"

Rev. C. Tobias Moberley, D. D.   Admission Free
Open 8:00 P.M.

After another quarter-mile or so a dirt road angled to the left, with a crudely lettered sign nailed to a post:

CAMPGROUNDS
Transients—One Night
We Can't Take Care of Our Own

As Ambrose, spelling Lee at the wheel of the station wagon, turned in at the entrance, Emily spoke up from the back seat.

"Long's we got the night here, Brose, I aim to take in the services at that tent meetin'."

He glanced back at her, frowning. "Aw, c'mon, Maw. A buncha Holy Rollers?"

"Call upon the Lord God," Emily said, "and He will hear your voice. Don't matter when nor who with."

"Well, you sure ain't goin' alone," Ambrose said firmly. "Way them kinda people carry on. Foamin' at the mouth and talkin' that crazy stuff nobody knows what it means."

Ruby said, "I'm goin' with you, Maw," then added, "Lot better'n settin' 'round here doin' nothin' till bedtime."

*S*upper, cooked and dished up by Emily, was early to allow time to attend the soul-saving efforts of the Reverend Moberley. Earlier, Lee, tiring of ham and preserves, had driven into town, returning with lamb chops, cans of soup, and a store-bought cake.

Ambrose found Lee against the truck's tailgate, smoking but not enjoying one of the "de-nicotined" tailor-mades. " 'Preciate a favor."

"Name it."

"Don't like Maw and Ruby goin' to this Bible-thumpin' shindig alone. Supposin' I stay here, keep Virgil away from that booze, and you go along with 'em? Do it myself," he added, " 'cept I can't bear up under the branda shit them Holy Roller preachers throw at you."

Lee shrugged. "Might be interesting, at that."

While the two women were getting into go-to-meeting outfits, Lee donned the pants of one of his two hand-tailored suits and stepped into a pair of black-and-white spectator oxfords. He propped a hand mirror on one of the truck fenders and made quick use of shaving soap and his Gem safety razor. After wiping away excess lather, he applied an underarm deodorant and was opening a jar of Stacomb when Ruby came over to him.

Her face was freshly made up, her hair neatly coiffed under a blue cloche hat. Her gray mail-order dress showed only a few wrinkles and her high-heeled black shoes gleamed. Sharply conscious of this Yankee's muscular forearms and a strongly developed chest covered only by the tops of his BVD's, she watched him rub the pink cream into his hair and comb it into a smooth pompadour.

"Looks to me like all you're needin' now," she said, straight-faced, "is a little lipstick."

Lee gave her a sidelong glance. "All you need is a little less of it," he said, and handed her the mirror.

*A*mbrose, seated on one of the station wagon's running boards, refilled his coffee cup and was placing the graniteware pot on the still-glowing coals when his mother—tall, spare and ramrod straight in a long black dress—appeared. Every strand of her iron gray hair was in place, her cheeks were dusted lightly with rice powder, and the smidgen of artificial color added to her firm lips seemed unlikely to offend the Lord.

Her son said, "Gotta hand it to you, Maw. You're still a damn good-lookin' woman."

"A compliment with profane words in it," Emily said, "is no compliment at all. Least not to my waya thinkin'."

Ambrose missed seeing her pleased smile as she turned away.

*L*ee drew up the knot of a blue necktie, smoothed the collar of a white silk shirt, slipped into his suit jacket, and joined the ladies. Avoiding the wooded area between them and the bordering grounds, they walked to the highway edge, along that, then turned into the lot where the Church of the True Faith stood ready to provide salvation.

Dust-coated touring cars, roadsters, and a few small panel trucks were strewn haphazardly about the open ground. Judging from the crowd on its way into the huge tent, women well outnumbered the men: a dress-up affair, with only a sprinkling of dungarees, overalls, and linsey-woolsey dresses.

The strains of "Shall We Gather at the River?" from a wheezing organ poured through the wide entrance as Lee followed Ruby and Emily into the enclosed area. Kerosene torches gave off a harsh, flickering light and an acrid odor. Most of the rows of wooden folding chairs were already filled, although a section at the rear reserved for the "colored folk" remained empty.

A young usherette in a white dress showed them her teeth, said "Praise the Lord" flatly, and led them to three adjoining chairs off the center aisle.

The organist, a thin woman wearing rimless glasses and an expression of soaring rapture, finished the hymn. Seconds ticked away. The silence deepened as the crowd gradually quieted. Then a white muslin curtain at the rear of the tent parted and a man stepped onto the dais and up to the lectern.

He was a man in his late forties, a tall slender man, a man with a knife-blade face under a mane of silver hair, a man whose deep-set blue eyes blazed with hypnotic fervor. He wore a white linen suit, a white shirt, a white necktie, and spotless white tennis shoes. He held a large Bible with a gold cross etched into its white leather binding.

He was the Reverend Doctor C. Tobias Moberley.

He put the Bible down gently, turned up his open palms and slowly raised them, bringing the audience rustling to its feet.

"Let us lift our voices," he boomed, "in loving tribute to our Lord."

The organist struck the opening notes of "Rock of Ages" and the congregation took over.

Lee Vance joined in. Through his early teenage years, and at the insistence of his parents, he had sporadically attended services at a Methodist church on Chicago's North Side. He'd fidgeted through the sermons, but the beauty and majesty of the hymns had somehow stayed with him.

He glanced at the two women. Ruby was singing strictly by rote, her mind elsewhere. But not Emily. Her face had taken on the sheen of piety, her eyes glowing as she lifted her voice in praise of her Maker, serene with the certainty that when the roll was called up yonder she'd be there.

As the sound of the organ trailed off, Reverend Moberley said, "I ask that you remain standing while we bow our heads in prayer."

He took up the Bible, pressed it to his chest, and lowered his head. "Almighty God," he began in rich, sonorous tones, "in Your infinite grace and mercy, look down on this humble gathering of Your adoring servants. Bless them, O Lord of Hosts, lead them along the path of righteousness and into the eternal glory of Heaven. We ask this in Jesus' name. Amen."

The audience took their seats and Moberley opened the Bible. He had once confided to a nameless young woman over a bottle of rye in an Arkansas motel room that he'd actually read very little of the Good Book. "All you need to get by," he'd told her, "is a concordance, a loud voice, and the balls of a brass monkey."

Now he placed his hands reverently on the Bible, as though to draw strength from its pages, and began his sermon.

* * *

*F*aint sounds of rifle fire and the distant *ka-rump* of exploding mortar shells shook Virgil Lucas awake. At it again, them lousy Krauts!

A dark night. Cloudy? No moon? He groped for his Springfield, attached the bayonet, and dropped off the back of the troop carrier. No one around; his buddies had went and took off without him.

The faraway gunfire seemed to be coming from all directions, echoing, swelling, fading into silence, then back again. Like it was coming out of his own head, for chrissake!

A staff car stood a few yards behind the troop carrier. He inched cautiously up to it.

Empty.

A line of trees off to his left. Funny sound over there. One'a them Kraut machine guns?

Dead silence.

Crouching, rifle held low and leveled, he crept toward the black wall of trees.

"*W*hat does Jesus think of you?" the Reverend C. Tobias Moberley thundered. "Ask yourself that question. Then look deep into your hearts, see the corruption that lurks there! The lewd desires of the flesh! The envy! The greed! The thirst for alcohol—that Devil's brew! The evil thoughts that fill the minds of so many of you here tonight!"

He began to pace back and forth in front of the dais, brandishing the Bible. His voice dropped dramatically. "All this Jesus sees in you, my friends. And let me tell you: it saddens Him! He wants you to look deep into your immortal souls. He wants you to weigh the price of losing your hope of Heaven for your sins. He pleads for you to repent. To

97

come to Him. To sink to your knees and ask for His divine forgiveness while there is yet time. For there *is* time. Yes! Time to make your peace with Almighty God. Time to save your immortal souls from the fires of Hell!"

A young woman in the front row cried out, "Forgive me, sweet Jesus!" and sank to her knees, panting, eyes blank, lips drawn back into a rictus of ecstasy.

Moberley slammed down the Bible, peeled off his coat, flung it across the dais, stretched out his arms to the congregation. "Heed the call to eternal salvation," he roared. "Rise, ye sinners! Come forward, and find the peace that passeth understanding!"

A stirring, a ripple of movement throughout the crowded tent. Here and there, women were tugging shame-faced men to their feet, pulling them down the aisle to kneel together in front of the dais. Others started a frenzied twitching and jumping. Cries of "Hallelujah! Praise God!" rang out. A neatly groomed, white-haired woman went slowly to her knees and began babbling unintelligibly: a manifestation of what was reverently known as "the Tongues." Two men dropped to their hands and knees and began crawling in circles, barking like dogs.

Bemused, Lee Vance watched and listened. His reactions swung from fascination to disbelief and finally to cold anger. Unless somebody got up there and strangled that hypocritical son of a bitch, half the town would end up in the loony bin.

Next to him, Emily Dawson suddenly stiffened, began to shake. He glanced sharply at her. Her eyes were glazed over, unfocused. Traces of white froth touched the corners of her lips. Before Lee could put out a restraining hand, she was out of the chair and on her feet, arms folded across her breasts, eyes lifted heavenward.

And her voice rose loud and clear.

"O Lord, we beseech your forgiveness! Take from us this

truck and its many bottles of whiskey! It was not ours, but Satan did tempt us and we were weak. Free us, O Lord, from . . ."

Lee was on his feet. He slid an arm around Emily's waist, tightened it sharply, cutting off the spate of words. Three rows back, two well-dressed men in their thirties were staring at them.

Still in a mesmeric state, Emily allowed Lee to steer her up the aisle. Together with Ruby, they went through the tent flaps and on out into the open air.

Lee slowed, glanced sharply back into the tent. The two men were now on their feet and moving casually up the aisle.

"We got us a problem," Lee said grimly.

Keeping his arm round Emily, Lee turned away from the roadway and began walking briskly toward the dark wall of trees bordering the campsite.

Ruby said, "It's the other . . ."

"Shut up!" Lee snapped. He shot a quick look back over his shoulder. The two men were now out of the tent and strolling casually in their direction.

"Faster," Lee said softly. "But don't run."

A narrow opening in the wall of trees to his left marked a pathway. Lee led the two women toward it. He said softly, "You two go ahead. Give me five minutes; if I don't show up, tell Brose to head north a mile or so, then pull off the road and wait."

They reached the pathway, vanished into the heavy shadows.

Behind them, the two men quickened their pace, reached the opening. They paused, listening, heard nothing, then stepped warily into the blackness and moved cautiously ahead.

Lee stepped from behind a tree and slammed a fist against the first man's jaw, sending him sprawling. The second man yelled, "Shit!" and nailed Lee with a hard right to the head, buckling his knees. Before the man could follow up, the heel of a woman's shoe smacked him alongside the head. He reeled back, ducked under Ruby's second swing and was lunging at her when Lee shoved him off balance. The first man, now back on his feet, joined his companion and together they closed in on Lee.

Virgil Lucas stepped out of the shadows and sank the blade of his phantom bayonet deep into the first man's belly.

The twin blows from Virgil's fists knocked the wind out of the man and he fell heavily, gasping for breath. The second man wheeled, swung from the heels and caught Virgil squarely on the chin. As the stunned mechanic fell, Lee sank the edge of his hand into the side of the second man's neck.

The first man began climbing dazedly to his feet. Lee said, "Not yet, buddy," and decked him with a single punch.

In the charged silence Ruby and Lee stood alone. He jerked a thumb at one of the men, panted, "Get his belt and necktie!"

Ruby, asking no questions, did as she was told. Lee stripped the tie and belt from the other man, trussed his hands behind his back with the tie, and was binding his ankles together with the belt when the man opened his eyes, mumbled, ". . . hell you think you're . . . ?" before his own display hand-kerchief was jammed into his mouth.

Ruby had already tied the other man's hands behind him when Lee joined her. He rolled the half-conscious man over, gagged him, and was looping the belt around his legs when a hoarse voice growled, "Sonvabitch hit me."

Virgil Lucas. That blow to the chin had served to snatch him from the Argonne and back into the reality of an Oklahoma night. He was on his feet, teetering on unsteady legs and blinking groggily at them.

Lee said, "Virgil, you just earned yourself an extra quart."

*   *   *

"I couldn't get nothin' outta Maw," Ambrose Dawson said. "What the hell was goin' on back there?"

"I can tell you this much," Lee said. "We're not on out of here in the next ten minutes, we're liable to be behind bars. You and Virgil take the truck and follow us."

He walked over to the station wagon. Ruby was waiting in the front seat; Emily sat stiffly erect behind her. He slid in behind the wheel and started the motor, then turned to look back at Emily, her face a pale blur in the darkness.

"Mrs. Dawson," Lee said flatly, "till we get to Kansas City, you keep the hell away from God."

15

*D*uring the next two days they traveled only by night, heading due north and steering clear of anything other than back roads and country lanes. While Lee put the risk of running into a posse from Grossmont City as slight, at least a small amount of precaution seemed worth the effort.

On the second night they set up camp in a field at the outskirts of Oklahoma City. Once supper was out of the way, Lee took Ambrose aside, unfolded the frayed map, and pointed out their present position.

"It's time we swung east," Lee said. He indicated a thin line branching off the interstate highway. "Now here's a road. Seems to go through a lot of hills and only a few towns of any real size. Cuts down the chances of our running into a state trooper or some smart, big-city sheriff. When we get near the Arkansas line, we'll head north again and straight up on to Kansas City."

"Sounds right good to me," Ambrose said. "Sooner we get there and unload that booze, sooner I get back to where I belong. Walk into old man Willis's bank, slap down the money I owe the man, and git me back my prop'ety."

He gave Lee a narrow sidelong glance. "You sure you got somebody goin' to pay us the kinda cash money you said?"

Lee's jaw hardened. "You think for one goddamn minute I'd go barreling across half the country with that sorry excuse for a truck if I didn't know what I was doing? Not to mention the risk of having my ass tossed into a prison cell."

". . . Fifty thousand, huh?"

"And it could run a good sixty."

"And all you git's a thirda that?"

"You expect me to write it out for you?"

"No use you gittin' touchy 'bout it," Ambrose said equably. "Just aimin' to ease my mind."

He turned away, walked off toward the station wagon. Lee, scowling, opened a fresh pack of Sacketts, lit one and blew out a long streamer of smoke. Already he had a belly full of wet-nursing these hayseeds, saving their hides, digging them out of one stupid jam after another.

One thing sure: There'd be six feet of snow in hell before any of them got so much as a callused finger on a cent of that money.

No place on God's green footstool he could hide, the man had said.

It was to laugh!

Virgil Lucas leaned against the truck's radiator, tilted the bottle to his lips, and emptied it in three smooth swallows. He took a deep, shuddering breath, drew back his arm to throw the bottle into the darkness when a hand reached in, yanked it away.

"That, my friend," Lee Vance said softly, "is something you just don't do."

Virgil blinked at him blearily. "She's empty."

Lee bounced the bottle lightly on one hand. "What you do," he said patiently, "is stick it behind those bales of alfalfa. Why? I'll tell you why. Let's say whoever had this load of Scotch to begin with has word out he's looking for it. He hears that an empty bottle's turned up wearing that label.

103

Virgil, right then's when we'd be up to our Hoover buttons in trouble."

He tossed the bottle to the mechanic. "Take care of it," he said, gave the man a companionable pat on the shoulder, and was gone.

*T*he service station attendant screwed the truck's radiator cap into place. He wiped his hands on a wad of waste, came over to Lee, said, "Both cars gassed up and the Ford took two quartsa awl. Comes out to six-forty."

Lee handed over a ten, got back his change, tucked the three singles into his billfold to join the remaining five dollar bill.

Down to eight bucks. The Dawsons, collectively, had even less. And K. C. was a long way off.

Time he did something about it.

Welcome to
OKLAHOMA CITY
Pop. 182,000
Capital of
THE SOONER STATE

At 4:20 that afternoon Lee Vance, alone in the station wagon, passed the sign and entered the city from the south. The clutter of household goods once roped to the roof and running boards had been removed and left behind, along with the Diamond T.

His first stop was a genuine cigar store. He paid a dollar-sixty for a carton of Murads, asked the clerk a few questions, got back polite answers. After leaving the store, he stood at the curb for a moment or two looking at buildings, at side-

104

walks crowded with pedestrians, at a steady stream of cars rolling along paved streets.

The sights, the sounds, the smells of civilization! He hadn't realized how much he'd missed it.

He took a few deep breaths of city air, climbed back in behind the wheel. Opening a pack of Murads, he lit one, leaned back, and rested his heels on the instrument panel.

Not until he'd finished the entire cigarette did he start the motor and drive away.

16

GREENBROOK
COUNTY CLUB
Members Only

*I*t was a long, low building of red brick, fairly new and set well back from the street. Decorative green shutters flanked the windows, there were neat flower beds and four eager young trees in the wide swath of freshly cut lawn. A parking lot off to one side was dotted with cars, most of them in the high-priced field.

Lee drove slowly past the club entrance, pulled into the curb half a block away. He ran a comb through his hair, reset his hat at a jaunty angle, then opened the car door and got out. Reaching into the back seat, he took up a small, blanket-wrapped bundle, tucked it under his arm, and headed for where the money would be.

He turned in at the row of red stepping stones leading to the club's front door. Under the late afternoon sun, two rotating lawn sprinklers threw iridescent veils of water close to the path, but a bit of fancy footwork got him safely to the entrance.

Except for two middle-aged men in golf togs deep in conversation, the small, sparsely furnished lobby was empty. Lee noticed a partially open door to an office in the left wall. He went over, knocked. A deep voice said, "Yes?"

Lee put his head in. A silver-haired man in shirt sleeves and a pair of checkered plus-fours was eyeing him across a large, paper-strewn desk. A walnut plaque next to a Waterman pen set announced that this was Mr. Joseph Keith, club secretary. He said, "Good afternoon, sir. Is there something we can do for you?"

Lee blinked. No Oklahoma twang? He pushed the door open, went in. "My name's Vance. Lee Vance. I'm here to see a Mr. Rawlins."

The man behind the desk gave him a searching, shoes-to-hat look. Spotless black and white oxfords, a flawlessly tailored suit in charcoal gray, a white-on-white silk shirt. The four-in-hand necktie was blue, with a diagonal maroon stripe. A Panama straw, tilted a bit rakishly. In need of a haircut, but not all that badly.

And a Yankee.

But then so was the man behind the desk. He flicked a brief glance at the small bundle under Lee's arm, said, "You're not a member of the club, Mr. Vance?"

"No sir," Lee said. He smiled, added, "At least not yet."

Despite the mysterious bundle Lee was carrying, Keith seemed satisfied—probably more so by the younger man's appearance than his answers. "Mr. Rawlins," he said, "is the club manager. If you'll step out, go down the hall to your left. His office is just off the locker room."

*P*lacing the bundle on the manager's desk, Lee unfolded the blanket. One by one he stood four bottles of Edinburgh Highland Glen Scotch whiskey in the center of the blotter and stepped back.

Mortimer Rawlins, a tall, slender, deeply tanned man in his late forties, eyed them, pursed his lips. He picked up the nearest one, inspected the label closely, ran a thumb firmly across the printing. No ink came off.

He looked up. "I haven't come across this brand of Scotch since Prohibition came in." He turned, handed the bottle to the club steward, a gray-haired man in a white mess jacket with GREENBROOK stitched in green script above the breast pocket.

"Open her up, Andy," Rawlins said. "Let's find out what we've got here."

The mess jacket yielded a fold-over corkscrew. Andy expertly removed the cork, poured a few drops of the liquor into his palm and licked at them. He nodded, set down the bottle, rubbed his palm on his pants leg. "It's the real McCoy," he told Rawlins.

The manager lifted an eyebrow at Lee. "How much?"

"Twenty a bottle."

"How many more can you come up with?"

Lee spread his hands. "I'm no bootlegger, Mr. Rawlins. If that's what you're thinking. I only got hold of these because I helped a fellow I know out of a jam and they were all he had to offer in payment."

Rawlins eyed him steadily for a few seconds, then glanced over at the steward and got back a microscopic nod: the price was fair.

"Give you sixty," Rawlins said. "For the lot."

Lee shrugged. "They're worth my asking price, Mr. Rawlins. This gentleman just indicated that. But if twenty dollars means so much to you, I'll take your sixty."

The manager's lips quirked in the ghost of a smile. "I see no point in trying to knock down a man's price if he won't give you the courtesy of arguing a little."

He looked at his wristwatch, said, "Pay the man his

eighty dollars, Andy, I've got to get on home," and walked out.

"Wait here," the steward said, and vanished.

Lee moved over to the open office door. Beyond it, a few members were at the lockers, changing into street clothes. Three men, wrapped in oversized bath towels, were holding a heated discussion just outside the entrance to the shower room. In a far corner a four-handed poker game was in progress.

. . . "Here you go, sir."

Andy was back. He gave Lee four crisp twenty-dollar bills, gathered up the four bottles, and disappeared.

Lee remained where he was, idly watching the men at the poker table from across the room. A hand was played out, the winner shook a clenched fist triumphantly and raked in a modest pot.

As the next dealer began to gether up the cards, a locker door slammed and a club member, slipping into his jacket, came over to the table. He bent, said something to one of the foursome, got back a resigned nod . . . and Lee began drifting in that direction.

The summoned player got to his feet, picked up his money. Lee paused to light a cigarette. The player left. The dealer leaned back, began looking around the room in search of a possible replacement.

"Sorry," Lee said. "Wouldn't mind sitting in, but I'm not actually a member."

The mildly startled dealer squinted at him. Lee, smiling apologetically, added, "I only stopped by to visit Mort but he up and ran out on me."

"Any frienda Mort's," the dealer said expansively, "is a frienda ours. Come on, grab a seat and put your money out where we can get at it. Whadya say your name was?"

Lee told him and took the vacant chair.

*   *   *

*T*he Bismarck Cafe stood between an exclusive men's store and a billiard parlor at the edge of one of Oklahoma City's better shopping districts.

At a quarter to seven that evening, Lee pulled up at the curb directly across from the restaurant and turned off the motor. At that hour most of the shops were closed for the night, few pedestrians were abroad, and no traffic to speak of. He lit a Murad, leaned back in the seat, got out his wallet and totaled up the take.

Including the proceeds from the sale of those four bottles, he had come away with three hundred and twelve dollars—and a bonus of handshakes all around. Not a sore loser in the bunch—and not one of them with enough card sense to go up against the corner newsboy.

He put back the wallet, left the car and went into the Bismarck Cafe. Strictly high-class. Soft-spoken waiters in tuxedos, spotless tablecloths, linen napkins, sparkling silverware, upper-class patrons. Not cheap; his Wiener schnitzel dinner with all the trimmings came to three-fifty, plus half a buck tip.

And worth every cent of it!

*B*right gilt letters formed a graceful curve across each window of the double storefront:

WINDSOR BILLIARDS
Hours 10 A.M.—10 P.M.

Lee returned to the station wagon, opened the door, then hesitated, looked at his pocket watch. Eight-twenty. Now what? Rush back to where he'd left the Dawsons? Sit around listening to Ruby's complaints, Emily's homilies, and Virgil on the Jew's harp till the yawning took over and everybody turned in for the night?

He slammed the car door, crossed the street, and went into the pool hall.

Lee took a few steps into the wide, deep room . . . and stopped. Pool halls in hick towns were dingy dens of iniquity. Wall posters of ladies in tights or pugs with their mitts up. Cracked linoleum underfoot, battered brass spittoons, back issues of *The Police Gazette,* the stink of last week's stogies, and a fat slob in a dirty shirt at the cash drawer.

The Windsor? Deep-piled maroon carpeting, No Smoking signs instead of gaudy dames or second-rate fighters. A pair of slow-moving overhead fans circulated the odorless air. A Western Union ticker next to a large wall-mounted blackboard used for incoming baseball scores. Three billiard tables—one marked for balk-line play, six regulation pool tables, another two for snooker.

A couple of college types at one of the back tables were the only customers.

A tall, rather fragile-looking man in dark trousers, white shirt, black bow tie and a gray sports coat was watching him from behind a blond wood counter. He said, "Good evening, sir. Something I can do for you?"

Lee shrugged, said, "Fellow I ran into at Greenbrook was supposed to meet me here for a few games of eight ball."

"You're welcome to wait. Perhaps a bit of practice beforehand?"

Lee eyed him narrowly. "East coast?"

"Philadelphia to be exact. And you?"

"Chicago." Lee looked around the room. "A slow night?"

"Not for this time of year. Our clientele is largely made up of university students. Business drops off during the summer hiatus."

111

Clientele? Hiatus? From a guy running a pool hall?

"Long as I'm waiting," Lee said, "maybe I should warm up a little. Since you're not all that busy, why not join me?"

The owner hesitated, looked over at the two players deep into their game at the rear table. "If you like. At least until your friend shows up. By the way," he added, "I'm Dexter Lathrop."

"Lee Vance."

They shook hands, then went over to a wall rack to pick out suitable pool cues.

Ambrose Dawson finished lighting a cigarette, said, "Sure hope he ain't gone and got hisself inta some kinda fix."

"Not him," Ruby said sourly. "You was to ask me, he prob'ly run into some two-bit floozy and won't git back here afore sunup."

The strains of "Tipperary" from Virgil's Jew's harp came faintly from somewhere near the Diamond T. Emily Dawson, wrapped in two blankets and huddled on a mattress made up of a down comforter, was already asleep on the leeward side of a row of thick bushes.

A car with noisy tappets passed along the dirt road beyond the masking row of trees. Ambrose got to his feet, stretched hugely, said, "Well, I sure's hell ain't waitin' up for him," and headed for the truck's cab to bed down for the night.

Ruby stayed where she was. She shivered, drew the blanket close around her shoulders. A devil's brew of worry, doubt, and anger filled her thoughts. S'posin' they did git to Kansas City and got all that money. One thing for damn sure, that Yankee would up and try to grab it all. You wouldn't catch him handin' over no thirty, forty thousand dollars. Not to the likes of them he sure wouldn't!

And if he *didn't* get away with it? Brose'd go and buy his

farm back, prob'ly even buy more land, use the rest of his share fixin' the place up the way he'd been aimin' to do long's she'd been married to him. And not a nickel of it for one single thing she'd want. She'd go right on workin' her ass off, doin' all the chores, gittin' old and fulla wrinkles and nothin' to show for it. Maybe take a ride into Christi once a month, eat in a restaurant, go see some crummy picture show.

No sir. She was gonna git what was rightly comin' to her. One way or the other.

Lee Vance sank the four ball, was preparing to take his next shot when he suddenly swayed and grabbed the table rail to keep from falling.

Lathrop glanced at him with quick concern. "What's wrong?"

Lee straightened carefully, took a deep breath, let it out slowly. "Little dizzy I guess. Been a tough day."

"Perhaps," Lathrop said, "we'd better make this the last game."

"Might as well," Lee said, then added ruefully, "While I still have a few bucks left over."

He missed his next shot, and a few moments later Lathrop banked in the eight ball. Lee shrugged, handed over one of his two remaining twenties.

Lathrop slid the bill into an imported Gold Pfeil wallet, pocketed it. He said, "I usually don't do all this well, Mr. Vance. Just one of those rare times when the balls insisted on falling in for me."

"When you picked out a house cue instead of a custom-made stick," Lee said, "I was sure I'd end up owning the place." He grinned. "That was my first mistake."

They put back the cue sticks and had reached the door when Lee gasped, staggered, started to slump. Lathrop caught him, propped him up against the jamb, said firmly, "It's time we get you some help, my friend."

Lee freed himself, stepped away, shook his head. "Thanks, but what I need right now is air. Fresh air, and a lot of it."

He opened the door and said, "It's been a privilege and a pleasure to meet you, sir." He forced a smile. "And damned expensive. Good night."

The door closed behind him.

Julius Appleton was seventy-four and a bit hard of hearing. He said, "Y'see, I was out walking the dog last night. Gets me up 'round eleven, whining and carrying on. Seems she had to water a tree or two. We're out on Mulberry, about where she crosses Exeter, you know, and this car goes by like a bat outta hell. Anyhow, to make a long story short, just as it goes past, this here fancy wallet come flying out, lands in the street. Well, I couldn't make out what it was till I go over and pick it up. Had this card inside, with this address and a phone number. But I hafta tell you: There wasn't a cent of money in it."

"Somehow," Dexter Lathrop said, taking back his Gold Pfeil wallet, "I'm not at all surprised."

17

Clouds. Clouds forming a towering gray black wall along the southern horizon and sweeping swiftly northward. An occasional flash of sheet lightning flickered in the ebon depths. Gusts of wind swirled, died, came back to life with added strength. Within the last half an hour the temperature had dropped twenty degrees and the air had taken on a harsh, peppery odor.

From the rear seat of the station wagon, Emily Dawson said calmly, "Mr. Vance. We don't git us to the lee side'a somethin' in a hurry, we're gonna end up needin' all the help the good Lord can provide."

"There's a good-sized stand of trees up ahead," Lee said. "Would that do it?"

"Take a sight more'n trees," Emily said, "to git us through a duster worth the name."

They had left the Oklahoma City area early that same morning, taking the eastbound highway Lee had indicated the day before. After a few miles, the two lanes became barely more than a narrow dirt road. Farmhouses were farther and farther apart, with the parched fields around them stripped bare of crops and native grass.

Lee managed to coax the Ford's speed up a notch or two. He said, "I saw a couple of lightning flashes, Mrs. Dawson. Maybe the worst we're in for's a heavy rain?"

Ignoring the question, Emily settled back. She'd had her say; let this Yankee learn the hard way not to doubt her.

The station wagon rounded a sharp curve in the rutted road, passed a wooded area on the right . . . and Ruby, in the passenger seat, yelled, "Over there!"

FOR SALE

Inquire
CORBIN STATE BANK
Corbin, Okla.

Trespassers will be prosecuted
This means you!

With the Diamond T close behind, the station wagon swung off the road, slashed through what passed for a front yard, and skidded to a stop at the north side of a peeling white clapboard farmhouse.

Car doors banged open and the occupants piled out. As Emily left the Ford, a sudden gust of wind slammed her against the hood. Ambrose moved quickly to steady her but she waved him off.

"The pump's over yonder," she gasped. "Git them canteens out and filled up. And anything else'll hold water!"

Virgil and Ambrose yanked the two canteens from the station wagon and sprinted for the well. Lee grabbed a tire iron out of the truck's cab and ran toward the front of the house.

By now the sky had taken on the color of dull copper, the howling wind was nearing gale force, the cutting lash of swirling dust had dropped visibility to near zero.

Ruby, shielding her eyes from the dust, stood frozen next to the station wagon. Emily wheeled on her, snapped, "Move, girl! We gonna need blankets, botha them lanterns, and a fat messa towels."

116

Ambrose said triumphantly, "That oughtta do her!" and set the filled wooden bucket from the well in the center of the parlor floor while Lee, fighting the wind, managed to close and bar the front door.

The room ran the length of the house, with an inner doorway to other rooms at the far end. A smoke-smudged hole in the back wall marked where a stovepipe had been. The floor was littered with a scattering of junk: four empty wooden packing cases, a horsehair settee beyond repair, a wooden table with three legs, a decapitated rag doll, and on a wall a crocheted motto that read Bless Our Christian Home.

And settling over it all, a thickening gray fog the texture of powdered talc was coating skins, putting dark circles around lips and eyes, clogging nasal passages.

Raising her voice, Emily Dawson said, "Any'a you folks 'spect to go on breathin' somethin' 'sides dust, wet one'a them towels down and tie it over your nose."

Once everyone was masked and the lanterns lit, the five refugees bundled themselves in blankets and settled down to wait out the storm while around them walls shook, timbers groaned, window glass rattled in loose frames, and layers of dust thickened.

Lee reached for a cigarette, thought better of it, spit out a clot of mud, swore under his breath. Maybe Emily, with her pipeline to the Almighty, could let them in on how long this thing was supposed to go on. . . .

He slept.

The hours inched by. The storm gave no signs of letting up. Ambrose had nodded off, as had Ruby curled next to him. Emily rose, redipped her towel, replaced it, and went calmly back to sleep. The yellow light from the two kerosene lamps gradually dimmed and finally winked out.

Virgil awoke, coughing. Them Krauts and their shitty mustard gas! He adjusted his gas mask, stumbled to his feet, felt his way in total darkness along the barracks wall, down a short hallway until he reached a locked door.

The skeleton key was in place; he turned it, opened up . . . and a savage blast of dust-laden wind sent him reeling back. He caught hold of the jamb, lowered his head and fought his way out.

It took the better part of another two minutes for him to reach the far side of the house, around that, and clear of the full impact of the storm. He moved close to the building, stood there panting, while the damp towel covering his mouth and nose allowed his lungs to pull in something other than powdered clay.

. . . A band was playing. A military band. Playing clear and loud. Mademoiselle from Armentiers, parlez-vous? *And with the music the pound of marching feet. Him and his buddies! Marching. Marching row on row, arms swinging, eyes front, marching between lines of faceless people, between tall buildings. Yeah! Right up fuckin' Fifth Avenue!*

Virgil unbuttoned his fly and urinated.

18

*E*mily Dawson said, "There's a way'a eatin' in a duster so's you don't come up chewin' mostly mud."

It was an hour past sunrise. Everybody was up, wet towels had sponged faces and hands reasonably clean, and food was on the table.

Sometime during the night the gale had shrunk to hardly more than a stiff breeze, leaving a legacy of thin veils of dust still floating in the parlor air. The three-legged table was now propped against one wall, with the empty packing cases serving as seats around its available sides.

Emily indicated the five towel-covered plates. "Ham and corn pone," she said, "and give thanks to the good Lord for it. Now how it's done, Mr. Vance, is you kinda fetch her up with the towel still over it and sneak in a quick bite. And do your chewin' with your lips tight shut, else you gonna be gnawin' on a lotta sand the air in here's full of. Still some water in them canteens, anybody wants it."

They ate. Gingerly and in silence. The mechanic was the first to finish; he drank from one of the canteens, got up and was moving toward the door when Lee said, "Hold up a minute, Virgil."

They stepped outside. Lee said, "Don't go wandering off on me now. I want us out of here in a hurry and back on the road. So if you've got a bottle stuck away, make damned sure you keep it corked."

119

"You go rushin' things, Mr. Vance," Virgil drawled, "and we gonna end up with junk for engines."

"Meaning what?"

"Meanin' them air filters, I don't first give 'em a good oil bath, git ridda alla that sand in there, 'bout ten miles down the road's far's you gonna git."

"How long will that take?"

"Depends," Virgil said.

*L*ee took his place at the table, explained why there'd be a delay in leaving, washed down the rest of his sandwich, and lit a Murad. "I don't know about the rest of you," he said, "but that . . . duster? . . . was the scariest thing I've ever run into."

"Nature," Emily Dawson said, "ain't always easy to abide with, young man. In my day I seen rain come down like the Red Sea on Pharaoh's armies. I seen hailstones bigger'n mushmelons, snow higher'n the barn roof, wind fit to blow the Devil free'a sin.

"And then there's the grasshoppers," she went on. " 'For they covered the face of the whole earth, so that the land was darkened, and they did eat every herb of the land, and all the fruit of the trees.'

"Exodus: chapter ten, verse fifteen," she added briskly. "A'course them was locusts, but I'd match up a Texas grasshopper agin a locust just 'bout any daya the week. Even eat fence posts and the wash right offa clothesline." She smiled. "Like I just finished sayin', Mr. Vance, farm livin's no beda roses."

Ruby said sourly, "You left out a thing or two, Maw. Like wadin' through a couple feeta snow gettin' to the privy and cold enough to freeze the stones offa bull. Or go twistin' a messa skunks out from under the barn."

"You folks don't have to go back to that, you know," Lee said mildly. "Once that whiskey's sold, why not move into the city, buy a place with indoor plumbing and no skunks? Enjoy life for a change."

It was all an act. An act to lull these hayseeds into believing they'd actually get their cut of the take, that this city slicker didn't intend to walk off with the whole bankroll. He knew the suspicion was still there, in the occasional sidelong glance, an awkward silence, a slip of the tongue. . . .

Ambrose Dawson had had enough of Lee's subversive propaganda. "I'm a farmin' man, mister. I sure don't aim to go movin' into some town and set around on my backside resta my life."

Lee held up a hand. "Who's saying you have to? Why not put a hunk of your forty thousand—whatever it comes to— into a business? Open up a . . . furniture store. Get into real estate. But take a vacation first. Climb on a train, travel around, see the country."

"Alla the country," Ambrose said harshly, "I'm fixin' to see is a hunnerd and sixty acres'a south Texas. With my name on it."

Ruby bounced to her feet, furious. "You talk like you was the only one's *in* this family! How's about me and your maw here? Ever come to you how mebbe we'd like to wear a dress didn't look like two flour sacks sewed together? And what's so all-fired terr'ble 'bout us takin' a vacation? Just once in my whole life I'd sure like goin' *some*wheres. Other'n the Eastern Star picnic!"

Her husband gave her a pitying look. "Now ain't that a cryin' shame. Let's hear how many vacations you went on back when you was slingin' hash for a livin'."

"Brose!" his mother said sternly. "That's shameful."

Neither of them heard her. By this time both were standing face to face, livid with anger.

"Don't think I couldn'ta!" Ruby yelled, "had I beena mind to. Plenty'a swell fellas was always after me to go on trips with 'em."

"I—just—bet!" Ambrose said nastily. "Guys like that big-shot bootlegger, huh? What else he git outta you for them dollar tips? 'Sides a cuppa coffee."

"I climbed in bed with him!" Ruby screamed. "That make you feel better? I climbed in bed with *alla* them! And you wanta know somethin'? Ever' last one'a them could do it better'n *you*!"

He slapped her viciously across the face. She fell back a step, put a shaking hand to her cheek, and stood there, eyes blazing at him with pure hatred.

Ambrose turned sharply, stalked over to the door and out.

*T*he well's wooden cover, replaced hastily by Virgil the night before, had blown away during the storm. Ambrose reattached the bucket, lowered it the full length of the rope, then brought it back up.

Nothing except mud. Sodden mud.

Ambrose muttered a short bitter word, tossed the bucket aside, scooped up the nearly empty canteens, went to the station wagon.

"Liable to be a long time 'tween drinks," he told his mother, dropped both containers on the rear floorboards, then slid in behind the wheel, slammed the door.

Next to him, Ruby sat stiff and silent, her eyes averted. He gave her a sidelong glance. "Still mad, huh?"

He got back no answer, no change of expression. He said, "Go ta hell," started the motor, waited until the Diamond T reached the highway, then moved in behind it.

Emily Dawson calmly picked up her Bible and opened it to the Psalms.

19

*H*eat. Heat from a naked sun high in a cloudless sky, bone dry heat, heat inescapable and relentless. Heat flooding the fields, baking the barren ground, filtering through tree branches and curling the leaves.

Virgil down-shifted as the Diamond T started up a steep, winding grade. Lee Vance, bare to the waist, peeled the sweat-soaked towel from around his neck, mopped his face. "Last night," he growled, "we get a dust storm and freezing cold. Now we get fried—and not enough breeze to blow the lint out of a gnat's navel. What's next on the menu?"

He turned, looked back at the Ford station wagon, barely visible through a curtain of gray powder in the truck's wake. He said, "Pull over for a while, Virgil. Stretch our legs, give the Dawsons a chance to breathe something besides dust."

Virgil failed to respond. Lee glanced at him, caught the mechanic's troubled expression. "Now what?"

"Engine. She's heatin' up on us."

"So? Pull off the road, let it cool down."

The other man shook his head. "Can't do that, Mr. Vance. Not goin' up no hill steep's this one. Best git her over the rise, then let her coast. That oughta cool her off some."

"Up to you."

The truck continued its climb, finally rounded a curve. The crest of the hill was visible now, still a good half-mile away.

The growl of the engine deepened, sputtered, backfired twice, then with a deep-throated *swoosh* the radiator cap shot high into the air atop a column of steam and boiling water.

"Sonva*bitch!*" Virgil snarled. He twisted the wheel to the right, stopped the truck a few feet off the road, and switched off the motor.

Virgil came back to the truck, dropped the radiator cap on the hood.

Lee said, "How far can it get without water?"

"Day like this," Virgil said, " 'bout a mile. But I sure's hell wouldn't wanta wreck the engine tryin' it."

Ambrose said, "How's if we drain some outta the Ford?"

"Not," Virgil said, " 'less'n you want *two* dead cars."

"You could take the wagon," Ruby suggested. "Go hunt up a farmhouse."

Lee shook his head. "Can't spare the gas. Besides, we haven't even seen a fencepost for the past two hours."

They stood there, the four of them, staring thoughtfully at the radiator. Emily had remained in the station wagon, safely out of the sun and deep into her Bible.

A sudden thought struck Lee. "Hey! Between the five of us, maybe *we* could fill it!"

Virgil looked at him incredulously. "Six *gallons?*"

Lee walked away, came back. He looked at the ring of grim faces, the furrowed brows, knew his own expression must be mirroring theirs . . .

"Got it!" he said softly. He turned, strode toward the back of the truck. When he showed up again, he was carrying two bundles from the Diamond T's cargo.

Ruby was the first to realize what he had in mind. "No!" she wailed. "Don't you do it! That's our *money!*"

"It's money," Lee said, "if we can get it to Kansas City. Right now it's just something wet."

He held out a hand to Ambrose. "I'll need your knife."

Reluctantly Ambrose dug into a pocket, brought out a bone-handled jackknife. Lee opened a blade, slashed a long rent in the burlap and removed one of the bottles.

As Lee began prying out the cork, Virgil said, "Gotta tell you somethin', Mr. Vance. You go puttin' that alky in there 'fore the engine cools off, you li'ble to git her right back in the face."

"One way to find out," Lee said. He flipped the cork away, extended his arm to its full length, cautiously tilted the neck of the bottle over the open radiator and allowed a little of the liquor to trickle in.

An angry hiss, a bubbling sound, a tendril of vapor. But the liquid stayed down. Lee let a full minute go by, tried again. When nothing happened, he dumped in the rest of the bottle and reached for another.

One by one six quarts of the world's finest Scotch whiskey gurgled into the radiator. Ruby's expression suggested she was witnessing a lynching, Ambrose might as well have been watching bodies being pulled from a train wreck, Virgil kept wetting his lips and swallowing convulsively.

When Lee reached for the second burlock, Ruby had taken all the torture a body could bear.

"That's enough!" she cried. "You already used up six whole bottles!"

Lee looked at the mechanic. "How about it, Virgil?"

It was a struggle, but reason won out. Reluctantly Virgil said, " 'Less'n we git real lucky, Mr. Vance, no way a gallon and a half's gonna do it."

Lee slit the burlap sacking.

*   *   *

*T*hey reached the top of the hill. Once gravity could take over, Virgil shut off the motor and allowed the weight of the heavy vehicle to keep it moving. Half a mile farther on, the road curved sharply to the right and leveled out.

And there was the water.

20

*I*t was too wide to be called a creek, not wide enough to pass for a river. Broad bands of sycamores bordered both its banks, and the water was clear, cold, and free-flowing.

Once camp was set up a hundred or so yards from the stream and out of sight behind more sycamores lining the road, Emily and Ruby snatched heavy bath towels and bars of soap and hurried off, leaving the three men to wait their turn.

The rest of the day dragged by. The temperature held firmly near the hundred-degree mark; that along with the bone-numbing weariness left by last night's winds, dust, and cold blocked any notion of getting back on the road.

Supper was put off till nightfall and consisted of cold ham sandwiches, peach preserves and branch water. The day's heat had dug in and refused to budge. Stars and a three-quarter moon provided the only light.

Time passed. No one had much to say. Unnoticed by the others, Virgil took a half-filled bottle from under the truck seat and disappeared. Emily excused herself, settled into a corner of the station wagon's rear seat, folded her hands in her lap, bowed her head, and fell quietly asleep.

Since their quarrel earlier that morning, Ruby hadn't once

spoken to Ambrose. He'd made a couple of halfhearted efforts to smooth things over, only to get back a cold glare and an eyeful of the angry set to her shoulders as she turned away.

Ruby plunked herself down on one of the station wagon running boards, rolled and lit a cigarette (he don't like it, see if I care!) and glowered at her husband's back as he stood near the truck while holding a muted conversation with Lee Vance.

. . . Up and told her to go to hell! And that's where she'd surely be, he was to git back that stinkin' farma his. 'Cept he likely wasn't gonna *git* it back—not with that smart aleck Yankee around. He'd stick ever' last cent of that whiskey money in his own pocket and be gone like blowin' out a candle! Leave them with nothin' and a long ways from Texas. 'Less *she* could figger out some waya beatin' him to it. . . .

She was on her second cigarette when Ambrose and Lee ended their discussion. On his way past her, Lee said "Good night" pleasantly, sauntered over to the truck, climbed into the cab and closed the door.

Ambrose said, "Hey, Ruby. Best git you some sleep. Got us a rough day comin' up."

She looked through him.

His lips tightened into a cold, hard line. He turned abruptly, strode to the opposite side of the station wagon, yanked open the door, got in front, lay down and stretched out.

It left Ruby with one of three choices: make up with this stubborn son of a bitch, sleep on the ground, or spend the night sitting next to her mother-in-law on the back seat.

She got in beside Emily, slumped back, and closed her eyes.

* * *

*L*ee woke to find himself awash in sweat. He stretched, yawned, lit a Murad, shoved the cab door open and got out.

No one up and around. Moonlight, a cacophony of crickets, the murderous heat. Sweat trickled into his eyes, ran down his arms and naked chest, soaked the cigarette in his fingers.

Ruby watched him walk slowly past the Ford, head for the bank of trees and the creek behind them.

A leg cramp woke Virgil Lucas. Ignoring the pain, he groped for the half-empty bottle, made sure he'd capped it before dozing off, then slid off the truck's lowered tailgate and began massaging the knotted muscle.

A flicker of movement at the far end of the clearing caught his eye. He looked up in time to see a woman's slim figure disappear among the trees.

One of them French cuties. Virgil gave it a moment of hazy consideration, shrugged, opened the bottle, and took a healthy belt of Scotch.

Sure beat the hell outta champagne.

*L*ee kicked off his heavy clodhoppers, stripped to the buff, and stuck a hesitant toe into the moving water. Cold as an Eskimo's ass, but on a night like this nothing could be *too* cold. He waded cautiously into the stream, wary of probable potholes and sharp-edged stones.

By the time the creek bed leveled out, the water was up to his shoulders. He took a deep breath, dived in, swam a hundred feet or so upstream, then turned onto his back and allowed himself to drift with the current.

129

From behind him a pair of arms closed around his waist and pulled him under.

An insistent bladder roused Emily Dawson. Barely awake, she fumbled open the car door next to her and slipped out. The moon assured her no one was around to infringe on the privacy she needed.

She walked across the open ground and stepped into the narrow belt of trees bordering the road.

"The hell's wrong with you?" Lee panted. "Brose wakes up and finds us like this, he'd . . ."

"He ain't gonna wake up," Ruby said. "Way he sleeps?" She gave him a coy smile, sidled closer. "Hey, you ever do it in the water? I betcha . . ."

He shot out a hand, grabbed her by the hair. Ignoring her pained yelp, he yanked her face close to his. "You—damned—little—tramp! Come sneaking down here like a bitch in heat, all set to pound a hole in the weeds."

He pushed her away. "Maybe for two bucks you'd be worth it," he added contemptuously. "But not when it could end up costing me sixty grand."

"Why, honeybunch," Ruby said, burlesquing surprise, "you talk like you was countin' on takin' all that money for you'-self!"

The anger drained from Lee's face, leaving it an expressionless mask. "What is it you want, Ruby?"

Her mocking smile faded. "Mebbe," she said softly, "the same thing you want."

Their eyes locked, held. Then Lee turned sharply away and waded ashore. He bent, picked up his pants, straightened—and Ruby was there, reaching hungrily for him.

"Lee," she said in a small voice. "Please. Be . . . nice to me?"

She gasped as he caught her by the shoulders, jerked her tightly to him. His mouth sought out her parted lips. . . .

"Yay bo!"

Virgil. Standing there, grinning foolishly, fumbling at the buttons on his coveralls, ready to take his turn.

Lee panicked. "You bastard!" he snarled and sprang at the mechanic, fists swinging.

Virgil, bewildered by this unprovoked attack, backed off. "The hell's wrong with ya, Mr. Vance? I ain't aimin' to . . ."

A hard right caught him above the ear, buckling his knees. He staggered, backed off, and managed to avoid most of a flurry of punches without attempting to throw any of his own.

And then, as Lee let go with a roundhouse swing, Ruby jumped between them.

A deep rasping sound from the station wagon's front seat jolted Emily awake. Annoyed, she reached over, prodded her son; he stirred, muttered something, and the snoring stopped. She leaned back again, dimly aware that Ruby was missing.

Likely gone off to have herself a pee, Emily decided, and closed her eyes.

*W*ater splashed against her face. ". . . you hear me? Ruby? Damn it, look at me!"

She opened her eyes. Lee. Kneeling next to her, his expression a tangle of concern and impatience.

She wet her lips, thinking back, conscious of a dull throbbing at a corner of her jawline. "You hit me!"

"You walked right into it."

"I was scared Brose'd hear you two scrappin' and come tearin' down here."

"He still might." He rose to his feet, scooped up his pants. "And just in case he does," he added, "we'd both better be wearing something besides goose bumps."

He watched as she slipped into her dress, felt a stirring at his groin. A sexy piece of goods, this one. If Virgil hadn't come barreling in on them . . .

"I'd suggest you leave first," Lee told her. He smiled. "I know a gentleman's supposed to escort the lady to her door. But not this time, okay?"

Ruby said flatly, "You wasn't foolin'. Sayin' you was gonna take alla that whiskey money for you'self."

Lee eyed her thoughtfully. "I don't think I said that, Ruby."

"Oh you said it, all right. You gonna do it—and I'm aimin' to help you do it."

He looked at her blankly for a long moment, then awareness dawned and he grinned in ungrudging tribute. "So that's it! You follow me down here, peel off your clothes, turn on the charm, climb all over me. I fall for it, realize I can't live without you. So we grab the entire bankroll, don't bother telling Brose and Emily good-bye, ride off into the sunset together and live happily ever after. That how it goes, sweetheart? Just like they do in the movies?"

"Don't kid you'self," Ruby said disdainfully. "I ain't gittin' tied up with no fella don't 'mount to a hilla beans. No sirree. We git holda that money, we split it even-up. And right then and there's when I tell *you* good-bye!"

A determined hand kept prodding him. "Brose! Git up!"

Ambrose Dawson opened his eyes, rolled over, managed on his second try to sit up. His mother was standing at the open car door.

"Cut it out, Maw," he grumbled fuzzily. "I'm tryin' to git me some sleep. Why'd you hafta go wakin' . . ."

"Ruby's gone," Emily said harshly. "And that Vance fella with her."

What she was implying took a moment to sink in. Then he was out of the car, fingers digging into her shoulders. "You know that for a fact?"

"A'course I do."

"Where they at?"

"Mebbe down there," she said, pointing. "By the crick. Havin' carnal knowledge'a each other, you can be sure'a that."

He had already turned away, his face empty of all but a cold, dark rage. He reached into the car, snatched the battered 32-caliber Remington rifle from the straps at the underside of the roof, and strode purposefully toward the distant line of sycamores.

*L*ee finished lacing up his shoes, got to his feet. He said, "Okay. How would you suggest we go about it?"

"Don't fool with me," Ruby said impatiently. "You had that figgered out right off. What I'm sayin' is I either git me halfa that whiskey money or I tell Brose what you're aimin' to do."

Lee smiled. "And end up back on the farm?"

"If I got to, you betcha!"

*H*e was still a few yards from the line of trees when his foot struck against something, sent it skittering across the grass. He bent down, picked it up.

An empty whiskey bottle. Discarded by Virgil only minutes before.

133

*   *   *

Lee said, "Okay. Let's say we *do* take the money and run. You think Ambrose'd sit still for it? Not if I know the man. We'd be taking more than his money—we'd be taking his pride, his self-respect. And that's why he'd come after us, Ruby. Especially you. Me, he never did trust. But his loving wife? To do this to him? Lady, he ever caught up with you . . . he'd kill you."

She showed him a curled lip. "Brose'd never do nothin' like that. He's too crazy 'bout me."

Lee shrugged. "You could be right. But you know what makes it even worse, Ruby? You're just as crazy about him."

Ambrose Dawson, iron-faced, went past his mother, jerked open the car door, and shoved the Remington under the roof straps. He stepped back, turned to meet Emily's accusing eyes.

Before she could speak, Ambrose said harshly, "You ain't to let on you know 'bout any'a this, hear?"

"I'll not," she said icily, "close my eyes to . . ."

"Don't you back-talk me, Maw! You do what I tell you!"

"That woman," Emily said, "is profanin' the Lord's holy law. Down there in them trees, wallowin' in sin. Have you no . . ."

The truth burst from him like a cry of agony. "Listen to me, dammit! I can't lose that whiskey money—not after we come this far. I shoot him, there ain't no way us gittin' it."

Her expression refused to soften. "You must harden your heart aginst this jezebel, my son. You must cast her out as unclean. For it is God's will that an adulteress shall be . . . "

He cut her off there, his voice savagely contemptuous. "Shut up, damn you! You're a fine one to talk, alla them years

134

you was layin' up with that Brady Palmer ever' chance you got! So don't you go bad-mouthin' Ruby to me!"

Emily, stricken, fell back, put a trembling hand to her lips. "Your . . . paw. He . . . did he . . . ?"

"Yeah. Paw knew. You bet he knew. Same as I did. And it hurt him, Maw. 'Cept he loved you too much to go hurtin' you back."

Bitterness put an edge to his voice. "Guess Paw wasn't much of a man, at that. Else he'd a done what the Good Book says and pumped botha you fulla buckshot right up there in Brady's red barn."

For the first time he could remember, Ambrose Dawson saw his mother's tears. "I . . . fought agin it, Brose," she said brokenly. "Got down on my knees, I did, and prayed to the Almighty for strength to turn from temptation. But I was filled with the appetites of the flesh, and your Paw . . . he didn't rightly know how to . . . to . . . pleasure a woman."

Barely able to voice those last few words, she turned away, covered her face with her hands, stood there shaking.

Nothing changed in her son's expression. "I'm goin' to sleep," he said curtly, and got back into the car.

21

A cloudless sky, a blazing sun, stagnant air, the sapping humidity. All held over from the day before.

They had pulled out shortly after dawn, the Dawsons in the station wagon, followed closely by the Diamond T, Virgil at the wheel, Lee beside him. Earlier, the truck radiator had been twice drained and refilled to prevent any lingering odor of Scotch from reaching the wrong nose.

The terrain was still hilly, with the truck laboring up steep grades and teetering around sweeping curves in the narrow roadway. Farmhouses were few and far between, the only sign of life an elderly couple in an ancient buckboard drawn by a spavined brown mare.

The Ford rounded a sharp curve—and Ambrose stomped on the brake. Blocking the road was a clearly marked patrol car with a man in a state trooper's uniform crouched behind the hood and pointing the twin muzzles of a shotgun at the station wagon's windshield.

"Hold her!" a harsh voice yelled. "Right there!"

The truck skidded to a stop behind the Ford. A single glance was all Lee needed.

The dream was about to become a nightmare. For all of them.

"You!" the trooper—a stocky, middle-aged man named Hepler—called out. "In that truck! Move her over 'longside that car!"

Virgil pulled up next to the station wagon and shut off the motor.

"Ever'body out! Git in the road! Move!"

Blankfaced, they obeyed, with Emily—exiting the Ford with shoulders squared and dignity intact—the last to do so.

Earlier on, Ambrose and Lee had gone over what to do in case something like this should come up, and agreed that Lee would be the one most likely to save their necks.

And so it was Lee who now spoke up.

"What's goin' on here, Sheriff?" he asked, managing to sound plaintive. "We ain't done nothin'."

The question was ignored. "Turn around! Alla you!"

Resignedly, they turned to face the station wagon. Hepler, shotgun crooked under one arm, moved cautiously up behind them, used his free hand to make sure none of the three men was armed, eyed the two women briefly, and let it go at that.

Backing away, the trooper said, "Okay. Long's you do like I tell you, nobody's gonna git theirself hurt. Now I want you men to git over to'rds the back enda that truck while I git me a good look at her."

Lee showed him a baffled expression. "All we got us on there's a loada alfal . . ."

The shotgun came up. "You aimin' to fuss about it?"

They formed a ragged line a few feet from the truck's tailgate while Ruby and Emily watched from beside the nearby station wagon. Hepler took a spread-legged stance and leveled the gun at the alfalfa bales. "Okay, Pretty Boy," he called out. "Pile outta there!"

No response. The trooper's voice took on a coldly menacing edge. "You got five seconds, Floyd. 'Fore I senda double loada buckshot in after you!"

And then Lee understood. "Pretty Boy *Floyd?!*" he said incredulously. "You claimin' he's in there? No *sir!* We got nothin' to do with no bank robbers."

The lawman eyed him narrowly, took in the denims, work

shirt, heavy shoes, field hat. Sure looked like just another turd-kicker. And sounded like one, too. Nothin' you could rightly put your finger on, but yet somethin' 'bout this fella didn't add up. . . .

"The man's been seen inside a couple milesa here," the trooper said. "And it ain't the first time bank robbers been hid out from the law by folks in these parts. Way they feel 'bout banks."

Lee spread his hands. "Well, then you go right ahead, Sheriff. Shoot alla the buckshot you wanta into them bales."

It was the ultimate bluff. Hepler stared at him searchingly, saw only the expression of an innocent man. His eyes went to the other two, found no trace of guilt in their faces. But somethin' 'bout that skinny fella kept botherin' him . . .

The hell with it; he'd already wasted too much time on these two-bit sodbusters. He turned away, hesitated, then turned back. Okay, he'd give it one last shot, see what happened.

"Start unloadin' them bales," he said.

To Lee it was obvious that the trooper was running a bluff of his own. Just reach for the first bale and the cop'd say forget it, plant his ass back in his car, and go pick on somebody else.

"If that's what you want," Lee said calmly and started toward the truck's tailgate.

"No!" Ruby screamed.

Sergeant Hepler placed the shotgun close beside him on the tailgate, selected a bottle of Edinburgh Highland Glen from the freshly opened burlock, and eyed the wooden expressions of the three men facing him.

"Wanta tell me," he said to Lee, "where you got holda alla this here whiskey?"

By now Lee had abandoned his good ole boy pose. "Does it really matter, Officer?"

"S'pose not." Hepler set the bottle gently next to the gun. "Guess I don't need gittin' into what comes'a breakin' the pro'bition law. Three-to-five years in the Federal pen can be real hard to take. 'Specially for them ladies."

He looked over at Emily. "My mother's 'bout your age, ma'am, you don't mind my sayin' so. And a fine, strong woman. But I surely doubt she'd live a whole lot longer, she was behind bars."

"The good Lord," Emily Dawson said serenely, "watches over them that believeth in Him."

The sergeant gave her an admiring half-salute. "There! You see? A good Christian woman, same's my own mother!"

He sobered, shook his head, muttered, "Just can't see how I'm gonna . . ."

Here it comes, Lee told himself cynically.

Hepler's expression cleared; he'd made his decision. He said, "Tell you what. Seein' as how my job's catchin' real crim'nals 'steada decent hard-workin' folks, I'm gonna let y'all git into that there wagon'a yours and git on 'bout your business." He beamed at them. "Now don't that beat goin' off to jail?"

It was Lee who put into words what the others were thinking. "What happens to the booze, Sheriff?"

The lawman gave him a small, faintly mocking smile. "Kinda su'prised you hafta ask, mister. Why, it's goin' straight over to the U.S. gov'mint boys. Can't tell—but I might even end up gittin' me a big permotion."

His blatantly dishonest smirk left no doubt that this was an out-and-out hijacking aimed at lining his own pockets. He said, "Hurry it up now. 'Fore I go changin' my mind."

Emily opened the Ford's rear door, reached in, slipped the

Remington from the overhead straps, and in one continuous catlike motion wheeled and fired three rapid shots.

The second bullet struck Hepler squarely above the right eye, killing him instantly.

*I*t took Lee and Virgil just under three minutes to get the body into the squad car while Ruby and Ambrose stood by in stunned silence. As for Emily, she'd retreated into the Ford's back seat and the solace of the Psalms.

Lee tossed the rifle in next to the corpse. "Give me twenty minutes," he told Ambrose, "then take off. The first sizable grove of trees you come to, pull over. If you don't see me, sound the horn once and wait. You hear what I'm saying?" he added sharply.

"I ain't gone deaf," Ambrose growled.

"I don't know," Lee said, "how they execute cop killers in Oklahoma and I sure's hell don't want to find out the hard way. So make damned sure you watch the back of your lap till this is over with."

He turned away, slid in behind the squad car's wheel, and drove off.

*A*fter three miles or so, Lee spotted a fairly dense stand of oak and cottonwood off to his right. He turned the wheel, bounced over a couple of ruts, rolled on down a fifty-foot grassy slope and through a narrow opening in the trees.

Once he was satisfied that the car could not be seen from the road, Lee cut the motor and got out. A squirrel scolded him from an oak branch; that and the relentless buzz of insects were the only sounds.

. . . Fingerprints. Using the dead man's handkerchief, he scrubbed the squad car's steering wheel, dashboard, and doors, followed that up with a thorough job on the Dawsons' rifle before shoving it under a pile of leaves. There was no way to trace a gun that old back to the owner, but hanging on to it could prove to be a deadly mistake.

He stood there, frowning. Anything else? Better not be; one slip and they'd be tying him a hangman's noose.

He shook off the thought, turned away, came cautiously out into the open . . . and saw twin lines left by tires on the grassy slope. Lines leading straight into the wall of trees.

A roadmap for anyone out looking for the missing squad car.

He was using a leafy branch to smooth away the tracks when the truck and station wagon showed up.

"Virgil and me'll take the truck," Ambrose said flatly.

Lee slid behind the wheel of the station wagon. That hick hadn't said ten words to him since they'd started out this morning. Nor to Ruby, come to think of it. Maybe he'd somehow found out his wife and Lee had been down at that creek last night and figured they'd gone there to pitch a little woo. If that was true, would a hothead like Brose just let it ride? . . . The Scotch! Had to be! No matter what, you don't start a fight with a guy who's about to make you rich.

He glanced into the back seat. Seated next to Ruby, Emily Dawson had out the basket of socks, squinting as she threaded a darning needle.

He said, "Mrs. Dawson?"

She glanced up, eyed him placidly, waited.

"The man offered us a way out. Why shoot him?"

Her steady gaze never wavered. "He was fixin' to steal from us, young man. For his own and personal gain."

"I know. But we're not talking about some Mexican bandit here. The man was a cop. What if he'd been on the up-and-up?" He saw her blank reaction, added, "I mean supposing he hadn't been crooked?"

She said patiently, "Like the Scripture tells us, Mr. Vance, whosoever shall obey the Lord's holy commandments need not fear His wrath."

The Diamond T took off. Lee started the motor and fell in behind.

Kansas

—:X:—

June 1932

22

TYLER GROVES TOURIST PARK
Tyler Groves, Kansas

Transients
One Night Only

An hour before sundown on what had been a clear, cool day, the truck and the station wagon passed under the wooden arch spanning the park's entryway.

Other than an abused '27 Autocar panel truck housing a young family of four, and a spotless '29 Lincoln sedan looking oddly out of place, they had the grounds to themselves. There were separate privies and cooking grills but no running water.

Emily had put together a meal of hot ham sandwiches and crabapple preserves, but except for Ruby—back to her old self since that night at the creek—no one seemed to have much of an appetite. An elderly, well-dressed couple came over from the Lincoln to visit, got a lukewarm reception, and soon left.

Ambrose sat apart, moody, chain-smoking, grunting a few words only when spoken to. Emily, acutely aware of what was troubling her son, had little to say.

Lee Vance polished off his helping of preserves, leaned

back, and lit a Murad. His thoughts turned to that dead cop. The more miles the five of them could put between themselves and the corpse, the easier Lee would be able to breathe. On top of that, the killing would likely be blamed on Pretty Boy Floyd; the law had known he'd been around at the time, and adding another killing to his credit wouldn't keep the guy up nights.

Darkness settled in. Night noises and light from a crescent moon took over. Emily hid a yawn, excused herself and slipped into the station wagon's back seat.

Ambrose got to his feet. "Gonna take me a walk," he said abruptly. "Mebbe go into town, hunt me up a picture show or somethin'."

"Why on earth would you wanta do that?" Ruby said.

"Beats sittin' 'round here goin' nuts."

"I'd go with you," Ruby said, " 'cept I ain't hoofin' it no four-five miles."

"Nobody's askin' ya to," her husband said evenly. "Might be a good idea you was to stay right here and git to know Mr. Vance better."

Letting that kind of remark go unchallenged could be a mistake. Lee said mildly, "What's bothering you, Brose?"

"Notta blamed thing," Ambrose said. He turned and walked off into the night.

Ruby looked nervously at the man across from her. "You figger he . . ." She stopped short when he put a quick finger to his lips and tilted his head toward the Ford.

Lee lit a Murad, shook another loose and held it out to her. "Just one," he said lightly, "and you'll never go back to Bull Durham."

Thin-lipped, Ruby brushed the cigarette aside, jumped to her feet. "I'm gittin' me some sleep," she announced, and headed for the front seat of the station wagon.

* * *

*L*ee awoke, sat up, stretched muscles cramped by the limited confines of the truck's cab. He dug out his watch, lighted a match, squinted at the dial. A few minutes past one: two hours since he'd dozed off.

Earlier, while passing through Tyler Groves en route to the campgrounds, he'd noticed a used car lot a block off Main Street and next to a lumber yard. Long as he was awake, he might as well go in and collect two sets of Kansas license plates to replace the Oklahoma ones he'd acquired from a similar source. The way cars—used *and* new—were selling these days, it could be weeks before the plates were missed.

He left the cab, slipped on his work shoes, tightened the laces. As he passed the truck he made out a blanket-wrapped figure asleep on the lowered tailgate: Ambrose, back from a wild and woolly night on the town.

*T*ilting his head far back, Virgil Lucas took four mammoth swallows of Scotch, then drew back his arm and hurled the empty bottle at the alley wall of Lenny's Auto Parts. He stood there, weaving, brought a second bottle from a deep pocket of his coveralls. Another pocket yielded a jackknife; he fumbled open a blade and began prying out the cork. And as he worked, he lifted his voice in song.

"Over there! Over there! The Yanksh are comin', the Yanksh are comin, the drum's rum-tummin' ever'where!"

It wasn't music, but it was loud. From directly overhead a window slammed up and a middle-aged woman in curlers and a flannel nightgown put her head out.

"You!" she yelled shrilly. "Down there! Git away from here! Decent folks're tryin' to sleep!"

Virgil backed off a few steps, managed to keep his balance, craned his neck to look up at her.

"Well now, ma'am," he called out, "I surely do ast . . . *ask* ya pardon. Mebbe I was ta come on up there an' hold ya nice'n warmlike, you'd git back ta sleep no time a-tall!"

The head disappeared. "Omar! *Omar!* Git on that phone and call the sheriff!"

HONEST HANK HARRIS
Guaranteed—USED CARS AND TRUCKS—Guaranteed
For a real bargain
Come see Hank

Pausing near the lumber yard he'd noticed earlier, Lee took a long, carefully casual look at the empty street. A few doors down, a black sedan stood at the curb in front of a two-story building marked Lenny's Auto Parts. A block to the south a street lamp showed a deserted intersection.

Forearmed with a pair of pliers from Virgil's tool kit, Lee strode briskly into the unlighted car lot, vanished among the dozen or so parked vehicles.

*T*he Krauts were there, all right. Likely no more than a small patrol sent to scout out the Americans' position. He motioned to his five buddies; rifles and bayonets at the ready, they dropped into a crouch behind a pile of masonry from a bombed-out storefront. . . .

A bucket-shaped helmet poked cautiously past the edge of the building, remained there for a full minute before a German infantryman, rifle leveled, stepped into the open. He stood there listening, heard nothing, made a beckoning gesture. One by one five enemy soldiers stepped out from behind the building corner.

"Fire!" Virgil bellowed.

Two powerful beams of light struck him full in the face.

A white Marmon sedan bearing the insignia of the Tyler Groves sheriff's office coasted past the car lot and stopped a few yards further on.

Lee edged nearer the sidewalk. Virgil was standing in the middle of the street, a hand raised to block out the glare of the Marmon's headlights.

The other hand was holding a bottle.

Car doors slammed and two young men in deputy sheriff's uniforms converged on Virgil. The blond one said, "Big night out, huh, buddy?" He pried the bottle loose, handed it to his partner, shoved Virgil not ungently against the car's hood, patted him down, found only a broken-toothed comb and the Jew's harp.

He stuffed both items back into Virgil's pocket, said, "Okay, fella, what's your name?"

Virgil, having been jolted back to present-day Kansas, gave him a bleary smirk. In a singsong tone, he chanted, "Name's Puddin' an' Tame. Ast me agin an' I'll tell ya the same."

The second deputy said, "Hey, that's pretty good. I'm gonna have to 'member that one."

By this time Lee, staying in the shadows, had worked his way close enough to see and hear most of what was taking place.

Virgil had become fuzzily aware that something vital was missing. Remembering, he said, "Hey! Gimme back that bottle!" and made a drunken lunge for it.

The second deputy, grinning, jerked it out of reach and only a quick move by the blond officer kept the mechanic on his feet.

"Don't go gettin' your pecker up," the blond said soothingly. "We wouldn't wanta jug a nice fella like you. Now whyn't you go right along on home, git to bed, and sleep it off?"

The other deputy was staring at the bottle's label. He said, "Pretty fancy likker you got here, Mister. How'd you come by it?"

Virgil showed him a curled lip. "Thass for me ta know and you ta find out."

"Made it yourself, I bet."

Virgil bristled. "Shows what *you* know! An' lemme tell ya somethin' else, mister. Got me a whole truck fulla them bottles!"

That earned him a scornful grunt. "Sure you do. Okay, where'bouts you got this truck?"

Nobody got out of bed early enough to trick Virgil. "Just you never mind where'bouts. I got her, thass all."

The blond deputy scratched an ear. The way rum-runners were clogging the roads these days, a thing like this had to be looked into. "Guess we better run him in," he told his partner. "Mebbe come mornin', we git some sense outta him."

Standing in the cover of a recessed doorway, Lee watched helplessly as the two deputies hustled the protesting mechanic into the Marmon and drove off.

*R*uby said, "We don't need him no more. Whyn't we just up and go on 'thout him?"

"Don't be a sap," Lee said impatiently. "He blows the whistle on us, they'll block off every road within miles of here."

Ambrose pounded a fist against a truck fender. "What we git for takin' a drunk on in the first place!"

Lee wasn't listening. He stood there, biting a lip as a tenuous idea began to take on substance. . . .

He reached out, grabbed the younger woman's hand, shook

150

it, said, "Congratulations, Mrs. Dawson. You're about to have a baby."

*T*he station house door swung hesitantly open. The blond deputy looked up from the pinochle game, muttered, "Well, lookee what *we* got," to his partner and stood up.

"Somethin' I can do for you folks?" he said.

Lee and Ruby, looking properly apologetic and ill at ease, came up to the countertop railing. He had on a pair of bib overalls, a dirty work shirt, and heavy dust-coated shoes; she wore a faded housedress, was overdue for a bath, her hair cried for a comb.

And to judge by her waistline, the lady was about five minutes short of coming down with triplets.

Nervously clutching his frayed straw hat, Lee said, "Name's Lee Dawson, Sheriff." Pointing a solid thumb at Ruby, he added, "This here's my sister, Missus Virgil Lucas." He was acutely aware of doing an uneven job on his cornpone accent but it seemed unlikely his audience would notice.

The deputy said, "Okay, Dawson. What's on your mind?"

"Well," Lee said earnestly, "it's about . . . 'bout my sister's husban'. We been layin' over couple miles outside'a town, y'see, an' Virgil—well, he up an' kinda wandered off, I guess you'd call it. Had them two bottlesa likker the man give him, and we . . ."

The other deputy said sharply, "Hold up a minute, mister!" He left his chair, came over to the railing. "Ma'am? Your husband a skinny fella? 'Bout six feet, big nose on him?"

"Why, yessir," Ruby said faintly. "That's Virgil. Has he . . ."

The deputy put up a hand, cutting her off, and turned to Lee. "Where'd he git this bottle, agin?"

"This fella," Lee said. "We was headin' for Topeka—got kinfolk there, y'see—and we come on this big La Salle.

151

Wouldn't go for sour apples. Virgil's real good when it comes to engines, so he got her runnin', and this fella, he up and gives him fi' dollars and them two bottles outta the trunk."

The blond prodded his colleague's arm. "Know what, Bob? Musta been 'trunk' he said—not 'truck.' "

It sounded plausible, but Bob was not a man to be easily convinced. He said. "Mebbe yes and mebbe no." His eyes went back to Lee. "How many'a them bottles would you say was in that trunk?"

"Didn't see for myself," Lee told him. "I was settin' in the car. . . . You seen Virgil, Sheriff?"

The blond officer said, "He's layin' in one'a the cells back there. Drunker'n a hoot owl."

Lee sighed. "S'pose we mighta known." Then a possible way out came to him. "Mebbe we was to pay his fine? Not that we got much in the way'a money, but . . ."

His voice trailed off. Bob was already shaking his head. "Nope. Gotta ask him some questions 'bout this fella drivin' that La Salle. You people come by in the mornin' and we'll let you know."

One option left. A long shot shakily based on what he'd seen and heard on this jinxed cross-country tour: Posted signs reading, "We can't take care of our own." Paths suddenly changed to avoid being panhandled by rootless victims of the times. Blank stares at these aliens from another planet. Look at 'em; probably ain't had a bath in weeks!

So, when there's no straws to grasp, you have to look for cobwebs.

Lee's shoulders sagged in surrender. "We'll be by 'bout sunup," he said, turning away. "And we do wanta thank you for . . ."

He stopped there as Ruby doubled over, groaned, and clapped both hands to her swollen belly.

The two deputies stiffened. The blond one said, " 'S'matter with her?"

Lee, his expression showing deep concern, reached out to steady her. " 'Fraid that young'un ain't gonna wait a lot longer, Sheriff. We been figgerin' least 'nother couple days, but them pains been comin' on now 'bout half-hour apart."

Another groan, louder this time, and Ruby began to sag to her knees. Lee caught her by the arms, his expression panic-stricken. "Can't you do somethin' here, Sheriff? We ain't ones to go askin' for no charity help, only we gotta get my sister to a doctor fast."

The blond officer hesitated, looked at the other. "See you a minute, Bob?"

They moved out of earshot. The blond said, "Doc Barton's visitin' that daughter a'his in Ottawa. And the last time I sent one'a these floaters over to Doc McKenzie, he like to bit my head off. Said the county's got too damn many hard-up local folks to look after as it is."

"Yeah, I know all that. But somethin's goin' on here don't smell right."

The blond said, "Then you better find out what. Or we both sure's hell gonna tangle with McKenzie."

Another groan turned their heads sharply. The woman was clinging desperately to the railing, her shoulders heaving.

The blond came back quickly. "Where's your car at?"

"Out there in front," Lee said. "We was . . ."

"Okay. We're gonna let him go. Now Selma Junction's just over the county line 'bout eighteen miles easta here. Take you no more'n half a hour. They got a hospital that'll take care'a the lady for you. Okay?"

"Okay," Lee said.

Missouri

—✕—

June 1932

23

Visit

America's Most Progressive City

KANSAS CITY, MISSOURI

50 miles

*I*t had been around three in the afternoon when the station wagon, closely trailed by the Diamond T, crossed the Kansas state line and entered Missouri. The weather had turned chilly, with a bank of dark rain clouds mounting along the western horizon.

Lee, at the wheel of the station wagon, lit a Murad and looked over at Ruby curled on the seat next to him. "You see that?"

Ruby, half awake, stirred, said, "See what?"

"That sign. Fifty miles to the Promised Land!"

"Kansas City?"

"Yep."

"Praise the Lord."

He muttered, "Don't *you* start that!" then glanced hastily over his shoulder.

Fortunately Emily had dozed off.

157

*T*he barber unfolded a checkered cloth, draped it across Lee's shirt front, tucked the edges under his collar, said, "First time you been in here, mister?"

"That's right."

"My name's Bert. How'd you like her cut?"

"Just a light trim," Lee told him, and settled back.

It was a four-chair shop located just off Wentworth Avenue. Only two barbers were on duty, with a customer waiting. A shelf along the rear wall supported a radio with a cathedral-type dome flanked by a dozen or so shaving mugs, the names of regular patrons lettered across them. The air smelled of bay rum and cigar smoke.

Bert got out a comb and a pair of long-bladed scissors and went to work.

A deep, solemn voice from the radio said, "During a speech today before the National Association of American Bankers, President Hoover stated—and I quote: 'The battlefront today is against the hoarding of currency. It has become a national danger; it strangles our daily life, increases unemployment, and sorely afflicts our farmers. If the vast sums of money hoarded in our country could be brought into active circulation . . .' "

The other barber, scowling, glanced over at the waiting customer, said, "Hey, Jake. Would you mind getting something else on there?"

After fiddling a moment with the dial, Jake got through to "Amos and Andy," cut down the volume, and went back to waiting his turn.

Bert, wielding the scissors with smooth efficiency, said, "Only way this country's gettin' outta the *De*pression and back to good times is we put us a Democrat in the White House. Now, I don't hold much with this fella Al Smith, him bein'

a Cath'lic and all, but you take this fella Franklin Roos'velt—
Presbyterian, I hear he is. Anyways . . ."

Lee closed his eyes and nodded off.

SOLOMON WISEMAN

*

LOAN BANK

Three gilt balls hung over the door. Behind the smeared glass
of the single storefront was a motley collection of suitcases,
guns, and musical instruments.

At ten minutes past nine that same evening, Lee Vance, a
cloth-wrapped bundle under one arm, walked past a bur-
lesque theater, a rundown rooming house, a honky-tonk
spraying barrelhouse jazz through its open doors. He stopped
in front of the pawnshop, tossed aside his cigarette, and
went in.

An elderly man in a gray pullover sweater looked up from
a newspaper open on the counter. "What'll it be?"

"I'm Lee Vance. Sol's expecting me."

The clerk gave the bundle a searching look. "Vance, you
said?"

"Yeah."

The clerk reached under the counter's edge, brought out
a telephone receiver, pushed a button. "Guy name of Vance
out here, Mr. Wiseman." He listened, said, "Yessir," put back
the instrument, and jerked his head toward a door in the rear
wall. "Go ahead."

As Lee reached the door, it was opened by a neatly dressed
man in his late twenties. He had a matinee idol haircut, restless black eyes, and the unmistakable bulge of a holstered
gun under his left arm.

From somewhere behind the bodyguard, a baritone voice said, "Come on in, Lee."

The bodyguard stepped aside and Lee went past him. In the small, plainly furnished office, a short, grossly overweight man in his fifties surged up from behind a kneehole desk and came over to throw a welcoming arm around Lee's shoulders. "How the hell you been, boy? Last I heard you were in St. Louis and Patsy Lucarno had sent a couple shooters around to see you."

"I wasn't in," Lee said.

Wiseman chuckled, waved him to a seat, and lowered his bulk back into the swivel chair. "Now what's this about a load of wet goods you're trying to peddle?"

Lee placed the package on a corner of the desk, slipped off the knotted length of twine, brought out two quarts of the imported liquor, said, "A present for you, Sol," and set them in front of the man behind the desk.

Wiseman eyed the labels and his lips pursed in a silent whistle. He picked up one of the bottles almost reverently, rubbed a thumb across the lettering a time or two, then set it back on the desk and glanced up at Lee.

"Seems I heard something a while back," he said mildly. "Had to do with a sizable shipment of Edinburgh Glen getting mislaid down South somewhere."

Lee said nothing. He went on looking steadily and without expression at the other man.

Wiseman's lips quirked in a soft smile. He said, "Finders keepers, huh? Okay. How many and how much?"

Lee told him the size of the cargo, then added, "It'll cost you seventy thousand, Sol. And that's a bargain price."

Wiseman rested his elbows on the chair arms, folded his hands, leaned back. "Make it fifty and you've made a sale."

"Sixty flat," Lee said. "That's it, Sol. I've got a couple partners to split with."

The fat man sighed, nodded. "When can I get delivery?"

"Tomorrow. Any place you say."

"Call me here. Around ten A.M."

*T*he young man in the freshly pressed uniform said, "Not around this enda town, no sir. Not 'less you're lookin' to get slipped a Mickey. What you do is go two blocks down, turn left, keep goin' till you hit Gower, then a block to your right. Place called New City Rest'runt. Tell Rocco that Ron Swazey sent you and he'll pour you the best drink in K. C. Food's good, too."

Lee gave him a dollar, got a snappy salute in return, and drove off. There was a lot to be said for a burg with even one cop like Ron Swazey.

*H*e dined on roast leg of lamb, washing it down with Columbian coffee the color of mahogany, topped it all off with a slab of cherry pie crowned with a generous scoop of chocolate ice cream.

Pushing aside the plate, Lee lit a Murad, sat back and gave the place the once-over.

Strictly high class. Furnished in good taste, decorated with a subtle flair, service that Chicago's Empire Room would envy. Not to mention the customers. Lovely ladies, both young and those well along in years. Gentlemen in tuxedos—even a few in tails. At the next table, a white-haired man addressed as Judge somebody was working on his third after-dinner highball.

From behind him a voice loaded with disbelief said, "Val? That you?"

His old nickname, long since discarded, brought Lee abruptly out of his reverie. A slender young man with curly dark hair and an olive complexion was standing across the table, staring at him.

Lee said, "I'm not sure I . . ." His voice trailed off as recognition dawned. "Tony? Tony . . . DiLucca?"

"Well . . . not lately, no. Now it's Anthony Dixon."

Lee gestured at the empty chair. "Park the carcass, boy! How about a drink?"

"Why not? Scotch would be fine."

Lee grinned. "Lately I've grown fond of the stuff myself." He beckoned to a waiter, ordered two drinks, then turned back to Dixon. "How long's it been?"

"Last I saw of you was the day they booted your ass out of Northwestern."

"Makes it ten years," Lee said. "What're you into these days?"

"Accounting. I'm a CPA."

Lee eyed the faultless cut of Dixon's suit, the white silk shirt, the thin gold watch on his wrist. "Must pay well."

"That depends," Dixon said and looked away.

The waiter was back. He set down the two highballs, added figures to the check and disappeared.

They toasted old days, clinked glasses, and sampled their drinks. That out of the way, Lee said, "Depends on what?"

"On who your client is," Dixon said.

Lee bent toward him. "Look, Tony," he said quietly, "if I'm getting too nosy here, let's change the subject, okay?"

Dixon took a slow deep breath, leaned back and crossed his legs. The dining crowd had thinned out by this time, with no one at the adjoining tables. "Hell, it's no big secret, Val. I'm in with the Capone mob. Do their major accounting, in fact. Reason I'm in K.C. is to check the books on a loan company Frank Nitti owns a piece of."

Forty-five minutes and two highballs later, Antonio DiLucca, aka Anthony Dixon, stood up and headed for the nearest phone booth.

162

FOR SALE
DAIRY FARM

60 Acres Fully equipped

Inquire
Central States Bank
KANSAS CITY, MO.

By the time Lee Vance drove past the sign and into the wide
driveway, rain was falling and the temperature had dropped
almost twenty degrees. As he pulled up near the front door
of the empty farmhouse, the station wagon's headlights
picked out the Dawsons, grouped under the front porch ov-
erhang.

Lee switched off the motor and headlights, ducked his head
against the rain and ran over to join the family.

"We come prit near givin' up on you," Ambrose said
harshly. "How'd it go?"

Lee looked past him at the door. "Where's Virgil? He'll
have to be in on this."

Ruby said impatiently, "Wandered off some place, drunk.
None'a this his business anyway."

Ambrose said, "Come on, willya? How'd you make out in
there?"

Lee kept them waiting while he lighted a cigarette, inhaled
deeply, and released a long streamer of smoke. He said, "Give
or take a few hundred, depending on the count, the man's
ready to pay sixty thousand for the lot. Cash on delivery."

Ambrose grabbed Lee's hand in an iron grip and shook it
roughly, Ruby cried, "Hallelujah!" and burst into tears, while
Emily held her reaction down to a broad smile.

"We done it!" Ambrose yelled. "By *God,* we done it! Sure
hard to believe, all we been through. When we gittin' it to
him?"

"Matter of fact," Lee said, "we're not getting it to him."

Their faces went slowly blank as his words sank in. Then

Ambrose took a slow, ragged breath. "Now you listen to me, you slick son of a bitch. If you fixin' to . . ."

Lee's temper slipped. "Shut your fat mouth, farm boy! I'm running this show."

Emily Dawson said calmly, "Might be fittin' for you to give us somethin' more to go on, Mr. Vance."

Lee put up a conciliatory hand. "You're right, ma'am. Just before I left town I ran across an old friend of mine. He gave me the phone number of a friend of his. I called the guy, told him what we had for sale. He's ready to pay eighty thousand for the load."

He took a final drag from his cigarette, flipped the stub into the rain. "Once we get it to Chicago."

24

*E*mily Dawson said, "Can't get the man to eat a blessed thing. Just lays there coughin' his head off and a'burnin' up with fever."

Virgil, huddled on the station wagon's back seat, mumbled incoherently, broke into a fit of coughing that shook the car, then sank back and closed his eyes.

"What he needs right now," Lee said, "is a doctor."

Ambrose gave him a look of sheer disbelief. "Just how you gonna go 'bout gittin' a doctor, one in the mornin' and a good fifteen—twenty miles from the next town? And say we do git him there, we gonna hang around till he gits well?"

Reluctantly Lee said, "We'll wait till morning, see how he is then. I'd suggest you ladies take over the front seat, get what sleep you can. Ambrose and I'll use the truck cab."

*D*awn was breaking when Ruby woke the two men. "He's gone agin," she said.

*A*mbrose found the body at the side of the road nearly two miles from where they'd stopped for the night.

KINGSBRIDGE, MO.
Pop. 472

Lawrence M. Barlow, M.D., was powerfully built, middle-aged, and a dedicated vegetarian. He was also the county coroner, owner of the Kingsbridge general store, and the town's sole physician.

He re-entered the office, sat down behind his desk, moved the lamp for an unimpeded view of his two visitors. He said, "Not the first dead hitchhiker I've seen and by no means the first not carrying anything with his name on it. I will say it was mighty nice'a you folks to fetch in the dead body of a total stranger. Not many people would've been willing to do a thing like that."

Emily Dawson said, "He was one'a the good Lord's precious children. Wouldn't be fittin' we was to turn out backs on him."

Doctor Barlow nodded to that. "Hard to tell how long he'd been out there, this cold weather and all. What took him off, I'd say, was galloping pneumonia. Not surprising; man was in bad shape to start with. Undernourished, and going by the ruptured veins in his cheeks and nose, a heavy drinker.

"Plus," Dr. Barlow continued, "he's got what looked to me like shrapnel scars. That'd make him a war vet. I'd not be at all surprised to learn he'd got himself gassed one time or 'nother. An autopsy would tell us that but there's no reason to do one."

Lee said, "Anything more you'd like us to do, Doctor?"

Barlow shook his head and stood up. "Nothing comes to mind, no. He'll get buried in the potter's field section of our cemetery. Another unknown man in an unmarked grave. Sort of a symbol, you might say, of the times."

"Like to think," Emily said, "when that comes to pass, some good Christian person'll say a prayer for the young man's immortal soul."

"You can be sure of it," Barlow said. He opened the office door for them. "One thing I'll say for Reverend Golightly: He wouldn't let an out-and-out heathen go to his grave unblessed."

Illinois

—✕—

June 1932

25

City Limits
Cicero, Ill.
Pop. 68,000

*L*ee Vance said, "Make a right at the next corner and pull up."

Ambrose, at the wheel of the Diamond T, nodded. White lettering on a blue background read Stokes Avenue. He made the turn and the truck rolled to a stop as Ruby, driving the station wagon, drew up behind it.

A sparsely settled area, mostly residential. Lee got out, moved over to the intersection's street light, took out a slip of paper, reviewed the directions given him earlier. He nodded, pocketed the paper, came back to the truck, and slid in next to Ambrose.

"Straight ahead another two or three miles," Lee told him. "Then a left onto Colfax. The warehouse'll be three blocks after that."

Ambrose, frowning, stared at him in the faint light filtering into the cab. *"What* warehouse?"

"Where we leave the truck," Lee said patiently. "I'm not letting it stand out in the street overnight."

"And we just stick her in there, walk off and leave her? That what you're sayin'?"

Lee held his temper. "That's what I'm saying. Listen to me. The place is run by the guy who'll be handing us eighty grand the minute he shows up tomorrow morning. Only we don't get a goddamn cent till he's satisfied nobody's trying to pull a fast one on him. To make sure, his boys'll go through the load tonight."

Even before Lee had finished, Ambrose was shaking his head stubbornly. "No sir! I ain't holdin' still for nothin' like that. Say we come back like you said, half the load's gone— mebbe all'a it—and then this fella up and tells us some crook busted in and stold it."

Lee gritted his teeth. This was what came from tying in with an idiot. He said, "I know what I'm doing. But you get a choice: my way—or no way at all. Go ahead, my friend, take your pick."

COOK COUNTY VAN & STORAGE
WAREHOUSE #1

The corrugated metal doors swung back to admit the truck, clanged shut behind it. A swarthy-skinned man wearing tan coveralls waved an arm toward an open space; Ambrose eased the Diamond T into it and shut off the motor.

The huge, high-ceilinged room took up much of the entire ground floor and was ablaze with light from overhead fixtures. Piles of beer kegs lined the walls; wooden cases of whiskey, gin, vodka, and assorted wines were stacked to the ceiling behind a padlocked steel-mesh gate. At a table in one corner three men in street clothes sat holding cards, waiting for the fourth to get back into the game.

Leaving Ambrose behind the wheel, Lee left the truck and walked over to the table. Coolly appraising eyes measured him; no one stood up, nobody greeted him.

"I don't suppose," Lee said, "Mr. Donatto is still around."

One of the players picked up his cards, eyed them, tossed three blue chips into an already sizable pot. "Up thirty," he said, then glanced at Lee. "Not when it's this time'a night, he ain't. Said you was to come back around eleven A.M."

The man next to him threw in a red chip, said, "Make it fifty."

"Thanks," Lee said.

He returned to the Diamond T, put his head in. "Eleven tomorrow morning, Brose. Let's go."

Ambrose finished rolling a cigarette, struck a match. "Not me," he said. He blew out a thin plume of smoke. "I'm settin' right where I am till you git back here."

"Now why would you want to do a crazy thing like that?"

"You oughtta know better'n to ask," Ambrose said.

The Harding Hotel ("A Radio in Every Room!") was two floors of whitewashed brick a ten-minute walk from the warehouse.

As Lee reached the lobby door, Ruby came out to intercept him. "Where's Brose?"

"Staying with the truck," Lee told her. "In case ten hijackers with machine guns show up. What're you doing running around this time of night?"

"Couldn't git to sleep."

"What about Emily?"

"Last I seen, she was soakin' herself in the bathtub."

"The diner next door's still open," Lee said. "How about a sandwich or something?"

"Awright with me."

The place was nearly empty. They took a small table in back, ordered hamburgers and coffee. Lee said, "I've got a phone call to make. Shouldn't take long."

He stopped at the cashier, asked a question, got an answer, and left the restaurant.

171

Ten minutes later, he returned to find his order cooling on the table and Ruby well into her sandwich.

They ate in silence, ignoring each other, until Lee finally shoved his plate aside and looked up at her. She was still sitting stiffly erect, holding her coffee cup between both hands and staring steadily at him.

He found his cigarettes, held out the pack, got back a small headshake, and lit one for himself. "Okay, Ruby," he said. "What's biting you?"

"I gotta know somethin'," she said. "Once you git a'holda that money, how'm I gonna git my half?"

Lee lifted an eyebrow. "Your half? Honey, as far as I'm concerned you don't get a dime."

She rocked back as though he'd slapped her. "B-but you said . . . that night. By the river."

"No, Ruby. You only thought I said it."

A rush of fury darkened her face. She said, "You know what I'm gonna do? Right now? Call up the *police* and they'll go grab that whiskey 'fore you can *spit*!"

"And spend the next three years in the pokey?"

That stopped her, but only for a moment. "I won't tell 'em no names. Just where it's at."

He was looking at her almost pityingly. "Kiddo," he said softly, "you're in another world now. Full of very unpleasant people. Pull a stunt like that and somebody'll come after you."

Her voice began to rise. "I don't *care*! Rather'n see you git it all, I'd . . ."

"I didn't say that, either." Before she could go on, he said, "Not that I wasn't planning on it. But then I found out something about myself." He smiled ruefully. "Seems I'm not a big enough bastard to rob people I like."

He stood up, dropped two dollar bills on the table, said, "Pleasant dreams, Ruby," and walked out the door.

26

Church bells woke Lee Vance shortly after nine. To him just another Sunday, to Emily an opportunity to take in a sermon before the family started back to Texas. And if he knew Emily, that station wagon wouldn't be heading out until services were over, a prayer offered up for Virgil, and a donation dropped into the collection plate.

He started to doze off, thought better of it, and rolled out of bed. A quick shower and shave, then into fresh linen, his best suit, the correct necktie and a pair of black and white oxfords.

The image in the dresser mirror nodded its approval.

Lee gathered up his two suitcases and descended to the hotel lobby. The bill for three rooms came to a steep fifteen dollars. He paid up without a murmur: after all, what was a lousy fifteen bucks to a man of means?

He found Ruby and Emily, both dressed suitably for church, sitting stiffly erect on one of the lobby couches. He gave them a dazzling smile. "Top of the morning to you, ladies. Long as we've plenty of time, how about breakfast?"

When Lee came in through the pedestrian door, he found an empty truck and Ambrose seated on the running board staring into an equally empty coffee mug. None of the four

173

men from last night was present, but the pair replacing them could have been out of the same gangster movie.

Ignoring them, Lee went over to Ambrose, sat down next to him, said, "What happened to the load?"

Without looking up, Ambrose said, "They counted 'em, stuck 'em on some kinda contraptions, and wheeled 'em outta here."

"Out of the building?"

Ambrose raised his head, eyed him blearily. He needed a shave, smelled of rancid sweat, and his bib overalls and blue workshirt were long overdue at the washtub. "How the hell would *I* know?" he snarled. "Nothin' I coulda done to stop 'em either way."

Rising, Lee walked over to one of the bodyguards. "Mr. Donatto show up yet?"

The men said, "Hold still," patted him down for a possible weapon, then tilted his head toward a passageway between twin towers of beer kegs. "Down that way and to your right."

"What about the stuff we brought in last night?"

"That you hafta ask Mr. Donatto."

Ambrose was staring sullenly at them from the running board. Lee crooked a finger at him. "Payoff time, Brose," he said.

PARNOWSKI'S GROCERY
Open Every Day
6 to 12

Across from the grocery and three doors down, Ivan Karnov, sixty-seven, finished raking the narrow strip of lawn in front of a three-flat. As caretaker for several small apartment houses on the block, Karnov prided himself on not allowing Sundays to get in the way of his job.

He had put down the rake and was reaching for the wheelbarrow when the grocery door opened and a young man, jacket collar turned up and cap visor pulled low, stepped cautiously out. He darted a quick glance in both directions, said something over his shoulder, and a second man about the same age appeared. They turned right, away from where Karnov was standing, walked briskly toward the next cross street, then suddenly broke into a run and disappeared around the corner.

The part about them running bothered Ivan. None'a his business, but it just didn't look right. . . .

The grocery door was half open. Ivan pushed it back, put his head in. "Boris? You in here?"

Boris Parnowski, blood streaming from a gash above his left ear, lay unconscious beside the empty cash drawer.

Giuseppe Donatto was in his mid-fifties with a rising crest of iron gray hair, a slight paunch, and a pair of eyes the color and texture of wet cement. The button of a hearing aid was screwed into one ear, with the wire running down the side of his neck and under the collar of a flawlessly tailored jacket.

Once his two visitors were seated in upholstered chairs across the desk from him, Donatto indicated a polished mahogany bar in one corner, said, "Little early I know, but if you'd like a drink . . ."

"Not for me, thanks," Lee said. Ambrose, sitting stiffly on the edge of his chair and clearly ill at ease, shook his head.

Donatto leaned back in the thronelike swivel chair, rested his folded hands lightly on the desk blotter. He said, "Not more'n five minutes before you two boys showed up, I get this phone call. What I was told, I'm sorry to say, is that it looks like I'm gonna have to back down on that offer I made you."

A second or two of stunned silence. Then, before Lee could speak, Ambrose was out of his chair and bending across the desk, his face inches from Donatto's. "Lemme git this straight, you sonvabitch. You sayin' you ain't payin' for that load?"

Donatto said softly, "Either you'll sit down or you'll fall down. Hard."

The eyes, more than the words, straightened Ambrose up and back a step. Then Lee had him by the arm, pulling him away. Ambrose hesitated, started to blurt out something, then yanked his arm free and sat down.

Lee returned to his chair, crossed his legs, got out his cigarettes. Donatto handed him a gold-encrusted table lighter, pushed an ebony glass ashtray within reach.

Lee lit a Murad, set the lighter back on the desk. He said, "Care to tell us why, Mr. Donatto?"

"Simple economics. This guy Roosevelt's gonna be our next president. Prohibition won't last six months after he's in. We just now get word the overseas distillers are ready to cut prices 'way down, trying to unload before then."

"That Scotch ought to be worth something to you."

Donatto gave it some thought. Finally he sighed, leaned back. "Sixty grand," he said. "And that includes the truck."

Lee glanced at Ambrose. "Well, Brose. Whatta you say?"

"I say *shit!*" Ambrose growled. "We coulda got that much back in K. C." He hesitated, shrugged in defeat. "Guess it's okay. Don't know what else to do."

Lee said, "It's all yours, Mr. Donatto. And thanks."

Donatto stood up, went over to a metal filing cabinet. He opened the bottom drawer, took out a large kraft folder, untied the string, and one by one removed six banded packets of currency. He tossed them onto the desk, retied the still bulging folder, dropped it back into the drawer.

"Sixty grand," he said.

Lee left his chair, picked up the money. "You wouldn't happen to have a large envelope?"

A desk drawer yielded one the right size. Lee tucked in the bills, sealed it, slipped it into the inner pocket of his coat.

*T*hey had reached the alley door when Lee stopped short. He said, "Something I forgot to ask him. I'll be right back."

He was turning away when iron fingers closed on his shoulder. "You," Ambrose said, "ain't gettin' two steps outta my sight 'fore we split up that dough."

Lee grinned. "Still don't trust me, huh?" He got out the envelope, shoved it into the deep pocket of his companion's overalls. "Then I'll have to trust you. Sit down someplace; I'll only be a minute or two."

Again he turned to leave, and again Ambrose stopped him. "Just a damn minute. I seen in a picture show once where a guy puts this envelope in his pocket, takes it out agin. 'Cept what he took out wasn't the same envelope."

Lee spread his hands. "And here I thought I could get away with it," he said ruefully.

Ambrose brought out the envelope, freed the clasp, turned back the flap.

The money was there.

*D*onatto handed over another two packs of bills from the same folder. He said, "How'd you get mixed up with that schmuck, anyway?"

Lee sat down, began slipping off his shoes. "I sort of like the man myself. God knows he's had more than his share of tough luck. Along with a wife who's ready to steal him blind and skip out. It's his mother who's got the balls in the family."

The man behind the desk watched him slide a pack of the banknotes into each shoe. "You really think this guy's smart enough to search you after coming back in?"

Lee said, "I wouldn't put it past him. Or blame him, either."

He stepped into the shoes, stood up, took a few steps,

chuckled. "Ten thousand a foot. Now I know what they mean by walking on air! In a way I hate to pull this on the guy." He grinned. "But not enough *not* to."

At the office door, Lee said, "I meant to ask, anything to that business about the distillers cutting their prices?"

"Not yet," Donatto said. "But it'll come."

They shook hands. Lee said, "Give my best regards to Tony DiLucca next time you run across him."

"You mean Anthony Dixon," Giuseppe Donatto said.

*T*hey left the warehouse and began walking along the alley toward the street only a few yards away. "The wagon's parked just around the corner," Lee said. "I suppose you'll be heading back to Tex—"

He broke off at the sound of running feet. Two young men, coat collars pulled up and caps pulled low, burst into the alley from a passageway between two buildings, nearly colliding with Ambrose.

For a frozen second no one moved. Then one of the pair yanked out a gun, leveled it, snarled, "Outta the way, you!"

Lee said, "Sure," caught Ambrose by the arm and drew him back. "Just watch it with that gun, okay?"

The man with the gun said, "Let's go, Mike."

Mike hesitated. "Hold on a sec," he said. "Lessee they got any dough on 'em."

Ambrose stiffened, hunched his shoulders. Suddenly aware that this crazy Texan could end up getting them both killed, Lee yelled, "Brose! No!" and shoved him back.

Mike circled behind them, began turning out Lee's pockets. He came up with the wallet, stripped it clean, threw it aside, turned to Ambrose . . . and brought out the envelope.

He ripped the flap open, said, "*Jesus!*" in a stunned voice, and held the envelope out to his companion.

178

* * *

*T*hey stood there, watching numbly as the two men raced to the street and disappeared.

In a curiously soft voice, Ambrose said, "So *that's* how you worked it out, huh?" and with a fury born of agony and frustration, slammed a fist against Lee's chin.

Lee staggered back, crashed into a corner of the building, and crumpled to the ground.

*R*uby caught sight of her husband as he emerged from the alley and came toward the station wagon. Something in the set of his shoulders, the way he was walking, touched off an alarm.

Seated next to her, Emily looked up from the Bible as her son reached the car and opened the rear door.

Ruby said, "Honey? Did you git . . ." The words trailed off as she saw his expression.

Ambrose thrust his shoulders into the back seat, dug through the space behind it and pulled out Lee Vance's two pieces of luggage.

Ruby said, "He stold it." It was not a question.

Holding both bags, Ambrose backed out of the station wagon, turned away, and headed for the alley.

*L*ee took two deep breaths, gathered his strength, then pushed himself up to his hands and knees, hung there as his vision gradually cleared.

Two closely spaced thudding sounds . . . and he was blinking at his luggage. He heard receding footsteps, glanced up in time to see Ambrose's back as the Texan strode toward the street.

On the second try, Lee was able to get to his feet. He propped himself against the warehouse wall, put a tentative hand to his jaw. That rube bastard packed one hell of a punch.

Still you couldn't blame the guy all that much. Sixty grand in that envelope, forty of it his. Losing something like that would upset a fucking saint!

At least *he'd* come out of this in one piece. And with his feet firmly planted on twenty thousand bucks.

Time to move on. He retrieved his empty wallet, brushed some of the alley grime from his coat and pants, adjusted his necktie, ran a comb through his hair, then picked up the two suitcases and walked up the alley.

Reaching the street, Lee hesitated. Now what? Thanks to those two-bit hoods, he hadn't a cent in his pockets. It being a Sunday, banks were closed. He could hardly waltz into some store, slip off a shoe, hand the clerk a grand and ask him to break it into singles.

Maybe he should've hit Brose up for a loan.

Two young men, coat collars turned up and caps pulled low, had materialized at the far end of the street and were running toward him. They were still half a block away when a police car, gong clanging, rounded the corner in hot pursuit.

The two crooks spotted a break in the row of store fronts and disappeared into it. The squad car screeched to a stop and two uniformed officers scrambled out and dived in after them.

Almost immediately, the cops reappeared, shoving the now handcuffed pair ahead of them. A quick search turned up a gun and nothing else of consequence. One of the young men passed a remark that earned him a knee in the groin. Then car doors slammed, the police car took off, and once more the street was empty.

Lee remained standing there, fingering his bruised jaw.
A gun. Nothing else.

*T*he break in the row of shops led to a littered cul-de-sac between a furniture store and an ice cream parlor, both closed for the day.

Lee paused, scanned the street while lighting a cigarette. A car turning into a gas station a block and a half away was the only sign of life. He wasn't surprised; at this hour of a Sunday morning law-abiding folks were probably still in church or making love or sitting around listening to the radio.

He stepped into the cul-de-sac. Shallow, no visible breaks in the brick walls. The only items of any real size were two battered metal garbage cans at the rear entrance to a hand laundry fronting on the next street over.

Lee took a final drag on the Murad, flipped it away, and walked briskly on down to the two garbage cans.

Both were empty.

It wasn't until he picked up the second can that he found the envelope.

*T*he Ford wagon turned in at the filling station. Ambrose drew up alongside one of the two gas pumps, turned off the motor, and got out as a young fellow wearing brown coveralls came out of a crevice-sized cubbyhole.

"Yessir?"

"Gas her up," Ambrose said curtly, "put in some water, and have a look at them tires."

"Yessir." Something's sure eating on this bozo, the attendant told himself. As he freed the pump hose he glanced curiously at the two women in the back seat.

The younger one glared back at him.

                              *   *   *

*S*tanding in the recessed entrance of a dress shop, Lee
watched Ambrose pace restlessly back and forth near the
station wagon.

He slid a hand under his coat lapel, patted the envelope.
The honorable thing to do was march over there, get out the
envelope, count off forty of those one-thousand-dollar bills,
shove them in that farm boy's mitt. No. Make it thirty-nine;
deduct one for that sucker punch in the jaw.

The honorable thing to do. And he'd do it, too. The minute
the pope got married.

*A*mbrose said, "Got a place 'round here we can git us somethin' to eat?"

The attendant stopped turning the gas pump handle to
point a smudged finger. "Next corner down, turn right a block."

Ambrose opened the car door, said, " 'Steada just hangin'
'round here waitin', might as well go git fed."

*L*ee watched as the Dawsons left the station wagon and
moved up the street in the opposite direction from where he
was standing. Where they were heading was reasonably easy
to figure out, it being dinner time. It would give him a chance
to clean himself up and plan his next move.

He picked up his bags and crossed over to the service
station.

"Yessir?" the attendant said.

"The people from that Ford?" Lee said. "Any idea where
they went?"

"Went over to that rest'runt on Kelton. Down a block, turn
right."

"How about using your washroom?"

"Help yourself. Right over there."

It was hardly more than a closet. Lee opened one of the suitcases, changed his shirt and tie, brushed alley dust from his suit, and rubbed down his shoes. By the time this was finished, he had come up with a way to keep from being stuck out here in the sticks: Call up one of his hometown pals and ask to be picked up.

He found the attendant in the cubbyhole office deep into a dog-eared copy of *Black Mask*. "Use your phone?"

"Don't have one no more," the young fellow said. "Boss says way business is these days, cost more'n they worth. But there's this drugstore three blocks down got phones."

"Wouldn't have a nickel to spare, would you?"

He got back a blank stare. Lee said, "Thanks all the same," picked up his luggage, and walked out.

He got as far as the sidewalk, slowed, stopped. This, his conscience said sternly, wasn't right.

Conscience? Oh, come on! The last time he'd heard from his conscience was on his eleventh birthday when he'd swiped enough money out of his mother's purse to buy that Daisy BB gun.

Remember what you told Ruby last night at that diner? How you'd found out you weren't enough of a bastard to rob people you liked?

Hell, that was just to keep her from pulling a stupid thing like calling the cops. Wasn't it? . . .

Lee turned and walked reluctantly over to the station wagon.

*T*he pump jockey was in the minuscule office and deep into his magazine. Lee eased the envelope from his pocket, slid out ten of the banknotes, hesitated. Ten thousand dollars? Give that kind of dough away? He'd have to be completely crazy!

He leaned in and shoved the bills under the socks in Emily's reticule.

*H*e had reached the intersection and was about to cross the street before he stopped for the second time. He set down the two bags, got out his cigarettes. He eyed the pack blankly, put it away, gritted his teeth . . .

He went back to the station wagon.

*O*nce more he dipped into the envelope. Once more he counted out ten thousand dollars. Once more he slipped cash into the reticule.

So it wouldn't be a total loss, maybe the old lady'd send up a prayer for the salvation of his shady soul.

His next stop would be the nearest nuthouse.

*H*e was at the juncture of the driveway and the sidewalk when a shiny new yellow Packard convertible made a screeching U-turn into the station, barely missing him.

The Packard bounced to a stop. A shapely blonde leaned out, said, "Hey, I *am* sorry! Didn't see you in time."

The attendant showed up. "Yes ma'am?"

Her smile was radiant. "The left front tire. I think it's gone flat."

"Sure find out for you in a hurry, ma'am."

"How *sweet* of you!"

The blonde looked over at Lee. "You *are* all right?"

"Never better." He came up to the car. "You don't mind my asking, you wouldn't happen to be a gangster's moll, would you? This being Cicero and all."

She laughed. Musically. "Now *that's* the most flattering thing anybody's ever said to me. Thank you."

The attendant was back. "Pressure's kinda low, ma'am. Could be a slow leak. I'll put some more air in."

"How *sweet* of you!"

By the time the tire was fully inflated, Lee and the blonde were into a low-voiced conversation.

The attendant went back to his niche. He heard the Packard's motor roar to life and looked up in time to see Lee toss his luggage behind the front seat and slide in next to the blonde.

The car backed into the street and took off. The attendant shrugged and went back to his magazine.